Also by Lorna Landvik

*The View from Mount Joy*
*Oh My Stars*
*Angry Housewives Eating Bon Bons*
*Welcome to the Great Mysterious*
*The Tall Pine Polka*
*Your Oasis on Flame Lake*
*Patty Jane's House of Curl*

# 'Tis the Season!

# 'Tis the Season!

A Novel

## Lorna Landvik

Ballantine Books · New York

Published in the United States by Ballantine Books, an imprint of The Random House Publishing Group, a division of Random House, Inc., New York.

BALLANTINE and colophon are registered trademarks of Random House, Inc.

Library of Congress Cataloging-in-Publication Data
Landvik, Lorna.
'Tis the season! : a novel / Lorna Landvik.
p.   cm.
ISBN 978-0-345-49975-2 (acid-free paper)
1. Celebrities—Fiction.  2. Self-actualization (Psychology)—Fiction.
3. Christmas stories.  I. Title.
PS3562.A4835T57  2008
813'.54—dc22        2008026637

Printed in the United States of America on acid-free paper

www.ballantinebooks.com

2 4 6 8 9 7 5 3 1

First Edition

Book design by Julie Schroeder

*To Charles, Harleigh, and Kinga*
*My best presents ever*

'Tis the Season!

From the "Here's Buzz" column in *Star Gazer* magazine,
August 7, 20—

The reason yours truly tips waiters so well is because
they often tip me. And ey-yi-yi, sometimes they tip *mucho
grande*! Ladies and gents, boys and girls, we were recently
handed a doozy of a document by one intrepid waiter
who works poolside at an oh-so-swank Beverly Hills
hotel. *The Pentagon Papers* helped bring down a president—maybe these *purloined papers* will help bring down
a gadabout heiress who's way too big for her size 4
bitches—oops!—I meant *britches*.

Here's the scoop: As you loyal *Star Gazer* readers know,
**Caro Dixon** has taken tippling to the nth degree, hitting
the sauce like an *Animal House* frat pledge. Our accompanying photo album documents her in all phases of dress
and undress, demonstrating why style and drunkenness
so rarely coalesce. (Is she doing on that yacht what I
think it is she's doing?)

Perhaps inspired by her many friends who've walked those recuperative twelve steps (rehab and plastic surgery clinics—home away from home for the oh so chic), our Miss Caro decided to skip a few steps and wrote (or *tried* to write) a letter of apology to those she's hurt because of her overindulgence in martinis, margaritas, and Manhattans. Now this is where it gets good and why I would earn a Pulitzer were the nominating committee hip to stories the people really want to read.

One recent southern California afternoon, Caro Dixon, slathered in coconut oil, lay on a chaise longue, writing furiously on a legal pad. Our plucky waiter took note of her scribe work, especially when the redheaded mega-heiress ripped the paper out of the pad and lobbed it into a nearby potted palm. (Let's applaud her for *trying* to throw away her own trash—people of her ilk usually leave that job to the help.) After she staggered out of the pool area, her towel dragging behind her like the train of one of her designer gowns, our waiter, curiosity piqued, casually extracted the crumpled wad out of the potted palm. What follows, dear reader, is Caroline Dixon's verbatim letter of "apology." Mee-ow!

> *Dear everyone I have ever supposedly hurt:*
>     *Silly me—I thought I was going to a party the other night at my "friend" Penny Englehart's to celebrate her*

new body (the boobs looked all right, although in my humble opinion, they could have tucked a little more tummy), only it turned out to be a gathering in celebration of a friend's one-year anniversary of sobriety. Which of course meant no drinks . . . and no fun.

Mr. Clean told everyone how much his life had improved now that he'd gone through rehab and followed "the program." I said the only program I care to follow is America's Top Model and only because I like to bet on the loser!

He yammered on and on and I tried to listen, but could I help it if I nodded off? Lectures do that to me.

Okay, so a week later I was in Biarritz, dancing with Andreas Stenapoulos, and I accidentally stepped on one of his two left feet and broke his toe. A couple days later I got caught peeing on Laird Wright's musty old yacht (note to his interior designer: is it my fault or yours that I mistook one of your decorative urns for a toilet?), and then at Princess Marlena of Austria's luncheon, I broke a teacup that Queen Victoria had given to her great-grandmother. She did not seem to find it helpful when I asked her if she'd ever heard of superglue. Not even when I said, "Das superglue."

Anyway, I realized that at all three of these events the common denominator was that I was plastered, and I thought, hmmm, should I forgo the deMarcos' cruise invitation and book a vacation at Betty Ford's instead? Then I sobered up and thought, "Nahhhhhhh, where's the fun in that?"

But I can apologize, and apparently that's a big thing in the "recovery program." So here goes. To those I've ever supposedly hurt: sorry. I didn't mean to do whatever it is that caused harm to you, but what can I say? I was drunk!

Besides, some of you deserve bigger apologies than I can give you. Penny—demand one from your plastic surgeon! Gina—ask for an apology and a refund from your acting teacher. Brad Somerset—whoever's responsible for your lousy personality, make them say they're sorry! My dear family—well, you're exempted because I know you don't believe in apologies, yours or anyone else's!

But I do, and in fact, I'm sure that all of you are sorry for hurting me. If that's the case, an apology will be taken into consideration.

Your friend, relative, employer, client, whatever,
Caro

Some show of sincere remorse, eh, people? Well, let's not be petty, folks. Let's send out to the poor little rich girl our best wishes for health and sobriety. Or not—why wish her something she obviously doesn't want?

HUDSON & ASHTON
ATTORNEYS AT LAW
NEWPORT, RHODE ISLAND

August 10, 20—

Dear Miss Dixon,

On behalf of Mr. Bradley Somerset, I am writing to inform you that a restraining order and/or charges will be filed should you make any further contact with my client.

Mr. Somerset requests the return of the engagement ring through my office.

Sincerely,

Arthur Ashton
Attorney at Law
AA/ws

## CAROLINE DIXON

*8/14/20—*

*Dear Arty,*

*Thanks for the day-brightener. I might have DTs, but your client has delusions if he thinks I ever considered that crappy piece of zircon an engagement ring. Give me a break—I've found better rings around my tub. And believe me, Mr. Bradley Somerset doesn't have to worry about any further contact from me—I'm taking penicillin right now to ward off anything I may have caught from earlier contact with him.*

*Have a nice day suing people,*

*Caroline Dixon*

August 14, 20—

Dear Meg,

Thanks for listening so long last night. You alone know what a hard anniversary it is for me to mark. (I can hear you now: "Then get out and make more friends to whom you can confide!") I'll take under advisement your suggestion to write the Kvitruds, but writing the letter isn't the problem. The problem is mailing it.

I look forward to your visit. Friends like you are treasures in this life of mine that is increasingly lonely. It's funny—I chose to be alone as a buffer against getting hurt, but lately I am finding loneliness brings with it its own pain.

Now I know for certain I won't mail this note either; I can't have you worried over what I'm sure is a passing mood— made worse, I'm certain, by the fact that I let myself run out of coffee. As you know, a morning started without coffee is a morning not really started.

Love,
Your whining friend,
Astrid

9:32 a.m. August 15, 20—
To: revbill@reacres.com
From: dfarms@azlinx.com
Subject: This weekend


Dear Rev:

Hope you've settled into your new retirement digs without too much hassle. Are you still wearing your collar on the golf course? No one would dare accuse you of cheating then. . . .

I'd love to visit Hot Springs and check out the new place, but not necessarily your new "cute" neighbor, so I'm going to take a rain check this weekend. I know it's Bev more than you who tries to arrange these dates, but please, Bill, I'd rather you find new ways to serve the Lord than my social life.

Anyway, Becky just foaled and I'm not about to tear myself away from the fun of these next couple days.

Cyril

# GILLIAN HEDGES

*August 17, 20—*

*Caroline,*

*Mummy and I were thrilled when your "letter" crossed the Atlantic and made an appearance in all the English papers! And then, what an added thrill to see the accompanying photo montage! How lovely to see Caroline ready to relieve herself on Laird's yacht! Oh, and look at Caroline coming out of Versace greeting the world with her middle finger! And there she is photographed in a knock-down, drag-out fight in the lobby of the Bangkok Four Seasons with Gina Whelvan! Need I tell you that all these thrills sent Mummy directly to her bed?*

*When is it all supposed to end, Caroline? When will you take "tormenting friends & family" off your to-do list? You're long past using "youthful indiscretion" as an excuse.*

*Also, in your "heartfelt" apology, I didn't read any mention of you stealing my tennis bracelet or Garrett Tyson. But I suppose if you listed all your wrongdoings, it never would have been published because you'd still be writing it.*

*Gillian*

## CAROLINE DIXON

*August 20, 20—*

*Gillian—*

*In my defense:*

1. *That urn looked an awful lot like a toilet.*
2. *You try to shop with thirty million Roman paparazzi surrounding you.*
3. *Gina Whelvan started it. She filmed a ninja movie this past spring and apparently likes to reenact scenes from it in hotel lobbies.*
4. *I'm only twenty-six years old, hardly ready to cash in my pension, but then again, what would you know about youthful indiscretions? You've been a senior citizen since the day you were born.*
5. *I never stole your lousy tennis bracelet, and believe me, I did you a favor by stealing Garrett Tyson. Besides, I read his wife's divorcing him, and if the prenup doesn't hold up, maybe he'll still have enough money for your taste. So go sic 'em, Gil!*

*Tell my mother and your mummy thanks for the support, as usual.*

*C.*

GINA WHELVAN

August 28, 20—

Dear (??) Caro,

My manager said to just ignore your letter but I coudn't so I'm writing back but it will only be this once Bcuz I realize to have you as a friend isn't really possible Bcuz your not a friend in the first place!!! A real friend woudn't try to sabatage someones career when its just starting to take off!! A real friend woudn't SLAP someone in front of all sorts of people including photographers so that the picture shows up in STAR GAZER with a mean letter! A real friend woudn't tell someone she's too dumb to find her way into a paper bag let alone act her way out of one!!! Not all of us were born with all your advantages, at least I'm trying to do something with my life besides drink and spend money and slap people who are supposed to be your friends.

Gina

## CAROLINE DIXON

*August 30, 20—*

*Dear Gina,*

*You sure know how to come across as the poor little wounded girl on paper—how come you can't come across as anything but blank on the big screen?*

*It's funny—you liked me well enough when I introduced you to your current manager, when I loaned you a car, when I paid for your pictures, haircuts, and even stationery! ("Gee, Caro, the letters of my name are raised and everything!")*

*Sorry I was born into wealth—like I had anything to do with that—and remember, you slapped me first.*

*C.*

September 2, 20—

Mr. Marcus Verlander
c/o Random House Publishing
1745 Broadway
New York, NY 10019
USA

Dear Mr. Verlander:

It is always with great excitement that I look forward to reading one of your books. I feel yours is one of the sharpest minds speaking on the political climate today.

However, I must express my deep dismay at *Feasting Through the Famine*. What sparked your radical conversion to such a harmful and egocentric consumerism? What made you abandon the ideals you outlined in *One World* and *The Real Gold Is Green*? Seriously, I could not have been more stunned if Gandhi had produced a war manual published by the British government.

Truly befuddled, I remain,
Astrid Brevald
No. 7
Flyngor Island
Norway

P.S. There are several typos; on pg. 37 *its* is a contraction and not the possessive; on pg. 178 *quantity* is used instead of *quality;* and on pg. 345 *Machiavellian* is misspelled.

From the "Here's Buzz" column in *Star Gazer* magazine, September 4, 20—

Need I remind you, dear readers, of all the upheaval the publication of **Caroline Dixon's** blithe and mean-spirited apology caused? Sources tell me she was barraged with unhappy messages from friends and relatives who think her apology borders on defamation of their character! And if her current behavior is any indication, she's no closer to taking the first step of the twelve than she was when she tried to fast-forward to step nine.

Last weekend she was at the Hollywood premiere of *Spanish Fly*, trying—by all accounts—to get the attention of **Alonzo,** the movie's leading man, and her former one (for about two weeks). Apparently drunken rich ex-girlfriends making horns with their fingers and shouting *"Olé! Olé!"* is not a flirtation the Madrid Macho Man considers attractive, for he quickly ran for cover, hand in hand with **Jacinta Flores,** the beautiful (and sober!!) actress.

Caro also showed up in London and was seen at Lulu's nightclub with her usual entourage—minus **Penny Englehart,** who's none too happy about having the work that was done to her tummy and chest exposed. Apparently, exposure isn't something that bothers Miss

$$$Bags, for she and members of her party gleefully lifted their tops as if they were at Mardi Gras hoping for some beads! (Some might ask—exactly how many beads is Caro's decidedly petite bustline worth? . . .)

## GILLIAN HEDGES

September 5, 20—

Dear Caroline,

I wish I could say I enjoyed talking to you last night, but honestly, I don't enjoy talking to anyone at 2:00 in the morning—especially when I'm talking to someone so inebriated I can barely understand her! Do you blame Mummy for refusing to talk to you?

I used to look forward to your return trips to London, but I was glad you didn't bother to stop in to see us—who needs the abuse?

Remember, throwing your life away is your own choice, but choosing to do so in such a public manner stains not only your reputation but that of your family. Your actions impact the memory of your father as well as the life of our dear mother.

Gillian

## CAROLINE DIXON

*September 7, 20—*

*Gillian—*

*I would like to officially inform you that all your duties as older half sister have been suspended. Please note the word* duties *(believe me, you've made me aware all my life what a duty it's been to be related to me) and the word* half sister *(it's you who always made that distinction to the world, quick to tell them that no, oh good heavens no, we weren't* whole *sisters).*

*Let's see, you were five years old when Mother married my father and seven when I was born. How did such a little girl learn such deep grudges? I can see where all the changes might have made you scared and resentful—but did you always have to take it out on me? Was I always* the bad guy?

*Was it my fault that my father's work meant we lived all over the world? Was it my fault you had to divide the year between us and your own father in England? Was it really my fault that the one lesson you tried to teach me all those years was that I shouldn't waste my time trying to force you to love me?*

*Well, Gillie, I think I finally learned it, and to your delight, I'm* sure, I will close this letter with the assurance that I won't bother to write, call, or contact you again. (As to you "looking forward to my return trips to London"—don't make me laugh. Your record of declining my invitations to get together vs. accepting them runs about 10–1.)

Caroline

P.S. You might be able to tell by the tone of this letter that I am totally sober. But not for long: I just ordered a bottle of Dom Pérignon from room service in celebration of the official split between the Hedges/Dixon sisters. I'll drink half the bottle in your honor, half in mine.

8:30 p.m.   September 12, 20—
To: mberg@cal.com
From: lw@wpalms.com
Subject: Communication


Dear Mitch,

I would encourage more e-mails; they seem to have more clarity for Sonia than your phone calls. (Although they are certainly appreciated, she usually has no recollection of them after she hangs up.) But she retains what's read to her for a much longer time, and whenever I print out your e-mails, she carries them around all day! I know that her eyes are too weak to read, but still, she'll hold them up to her face and repeat almost verbatim what I've read!

Your parents were here with her for the evening meal and they had a good time listening to Sonia "read" the letter from her Mitchie!

Sincerely,
Lorraine Welby
Family Liaison
Whispering Palms Adult Residence

*4:30 p.m.  September 18, 20—*
*To: dfarms@azlinx.com*
*From: revbill@reacres.com*
*Subject: You*


*Dear Cy,*

*Reverend Storby tells me you're making yourself scarce at All Glory. Give the guy a chance, Cyril—just because you've been spoiled by my fathomless wisdom, infinite grace, and fiery intellectual powers doesn't mean he doesn't have anything to offer!*

*I don't like thinking of you sitting at home brooding on Sunday morning. It's been a while since you were the first one at church, ready to greet all comers in that snazzy bolo tie of yours, and I know while a lot of the congregants don't miss that lousy cologne of yours, they miss you. "Especially the women," Bev says.*

Vaya con dios,

*Bill*

WORLD OF CHANGE
16 WEST UMBERTON
LONDON SW, ENGLAND

September 18, 20—

Dear Miss Caroline Dixon:

The board of directors at World of Change would like to thank you once again for your generosity toward our charity. Your financial assistance has helped us in our efforts to bring hope, help, and education to girls and women around the world.

While we hope your interest in and sponsorship of World of Change will continue, we have decided to change our advertising campaign, in which you played an important part. We will no longer be using celebrities in our fundraising efforts; we believe the charity is now firmly established and no longer needs "names" to draw attention to it.

Thank you for all your efforts on our behalf—

remember, it's up to all of us to create a World
of Change!

Sincerely,
Agatha Smythe
Director

## CAROLINE DIXON

*September 23, 20—*

*Dear Ms. Smythe:*

*So what you're telling me is that you think my association with your campaign is now a liability? I suppose you came to that brilliant conclusion after that lovely picture of me appeared in all the rags. FYI, everyone was flashing their breasts; they only chose to publish pictures of the good ones.*

*If one of your stated goals is to empower women, I can't see why a picture of me flaunting my glorious mammaries is such a bad thing.*

*In and out of B cups, I remain,*

*Caroline Dixon*

*P.S. Enclosed please find a check—I still think your program is great, even though its director is an uptight, hypocritical old priss.*

11:07 p.m. September 24, 20—
To: revbill@reacres.com
From: dfarms@azlinx.com
Subject: Re: You

Dear Bill,

Sorry I haven't responded with my usual lightning speed—I've been having a lot of fun with Becky and her colt. I can sit for hours watching that little bugger—he's already got a frisky little personality, and Becky's had to give him a couple gentle nips to keep him in line! I'm calling him Flipper just because he's so playful. (Maybe I am losing my mind if I'm naming a horse after a dolphin on an old TV show. . . .)

I hope I'm not hurting the Rev. Storby's feelings, but you know church wasn't giving me much even during your last year there. It used to be such a special place, but now . . . well, not to see Cassie in the bell choir, or have her elbow me hard when I put nickels in the collection plate . . . I don't know, how can it mean the same?

And I don't suppose God cares where I am when I'm

communing with Him . . . if I'm communing with Him at all.

Aw, don't mind me, it's late, and there's a sad song on the radio. . . .

Cyril

From the "Here's Buzz" column in *Star Gazer* magazine, September 25, 20—

Faithful readers, Wilshire Boulevard in Beverly Hills was nearly the scene of a bloody brawl as a Hollywood mega-couple **Romanda** (hunk actor **Robert Sherwin** and hunkress **Amanda Wyatt**) exited the offices of big-time divorce lawyer **Wendell Glen**. And who should be entering the offices at the same time? Hiding behind sunglasses with lenses the size of dinner plates were **Sherwin's** ex, actress **Ali Gennaro,** and *her* current boyfriend (and Amanda's ex–hair stylist), **Nick Davis**. (Got that?) Screaming, shouting, and a game of "Push the Ex" ensued, but fortunately, saner heads prevailed and the two couples parted before any royal Hollywood blood was spilled.

**Caro Dixon,** on the other hand, never lets things like saner heads get in the way of her fun. Recently dining at Rupert's in Malibu, Miss $$$Bags chose to express her disapproval at her clams on the half shell by throwing them across the restaurant and into the lap of French chanteuse **Chantal Mignon.** Canard à l'orange, haricots verts, and crêpes à la Normande flew before the beleaguered maître d' regained order. . . .

October 10, 20—

Jenson Foods
10 Strand Ave.
Glasgow, Scotland
UK

Dear Sirs and Mesdames:

While living in London years ago, I acquired a taste for your dipped shortbread cookies and have been ordering them through the mail for years. My quarrel is not with the taste—they are still as good as ever—but with the new packaging.

In this day of dwindling energy and resources, is it really necessary to package in cellophane each row of cookies? There are four rows in each box of Jenson Shorts, which translates into *a lot* of cellophane.

As a longtime customer, I can assure you I never suffered any ill effects from eating your *unwrapped* cookies!

I hope very much that you will return to your more sensible and less wasteful method of packaging Jenson Shorts.

Sincerely,
Astrid Brevald
No. 7
Flyngor Island
Norway

EAST BRIDGE PUBLISHERS
LONDON, ENGLAND

October 11, 20—

Dear Astrid,

Is my guest bed made up? Are you fully stocked with that goat cheese I love? A nice little bottle of aquavit? Good, then we shall be all set.

I'm bringing much work for you, but I expect we should ignore most of it in favor of long walks on the beach, lovely chats by the fire, and, of course, frequent toasts with said aquavit. Is your handsome Nordic postman still on the job? I look forward to seeing him; Alex has assured me that looking is acceptable as long as I don't undress anyone with my eyes.

See you soon!

Meg

*You and a guest*
*are cordially invited to*

*Caroline Dixon's*
*annual Halloween bash!*

*This year we'll be celebrating at*
*my home in Malibu, California.*

*Join me for a weekend of*
*tricking and treating!*

*Hope to see you there—boo!*

*RSVP*

*Name:* ___Penelope Englehart___

*I will be coming—stock the fridge!* __

*I can't make it, and I'm bummed!* __X__

*P.S.: I and my false bosoms are already previously engaged.*

*Name:* Mr. and Mrs. Laird Wright

*I will be coming—stock the fridge!* __

*I can't make it, and I'm bummed!* X

P.S.: Laird and I will be in the Caribbean on our "musty yacht" (recently disinfected).

Name: _____ Gina Whelvan _____

*I will be coming—stock the fridge!* ___

*I can't make it, and I'm bummed!* X

Only I'm not bummed! —Gina

from the desk of
KATHY

10/11/20—

Re: Halloween Party

Caro—

I just got the latest RSVPs—eighteen more people have declined, and we're waiting for five more responses . . . should we cancel the whole thing?

Please advise.

From the "Here's Buzz" column in *Star Gazer* magazine, October 16, 20—

Since she was twenty-one (and of legal age), **Caro Dixon** has hosted a huge, weekend-long Halloween bash. Past invitees say it's taken weeks to recover from the hangover as well as the debauchery! (Equal parts tricks *and* treats.) It's been one of the most coveted invitations of the year . . . until this year, when friends and acquaintances, tired of the antics of our favorite heiress-on-a-bender, have virtually boycotted the event. Sources tell me the RSVPs are all coming back marked "Thanks but no thanks"!

THE RYLAND HOTEL
MIAMI, FLORIDA


October 17, 20—

Mr. Ernst Lalley
Lalley & Associates
9200 Sunset Blvd.
Los Angeles, CA 90069

Dear Mr. Lalley,

Enclosed please find a bill in the amount of $12,745.00 for damages done (itemization attached) by your client, Ms. Caroline Dixon, while she was a guest here from October 27 to October 31.

Timely remittance will be appreciated.

Sincerely,

Dorian Albrecht
Guest Relations

from the desk of
KATHY

10/20/20—

Geez, Caro, where are you? Since I don't know how to reach you and have no idea where you are, I'm putting this note on your desk in the hopes that you might swing by home one of these days. It's so hard to track you down—do you know you can actually pick up your cell phone and talk to the person on the other end of the line? Could you *please* check in with me a little more often? And maybe when you're *not* drinking?

Please see attached the copy of the lease agreement to the house in Aspen. Please note that Mr. Lalley has highlighted the parts of the agreement in dispute. He says the Irvines are legally entitled to break the lease because of the smashed tiles in the guest house and the tread marks on the lawn. Also enclosed are bills from the Ryland Hotel and Club 74. He says he's paid them but wants you to see in black and white the "cause and effect" of your actions.

Call me.

Kathy

From the "Here's Buzz" column in *Star Gazer* magazine,
October 23, 20—

Any of my faithful readers tune into other media to
hear yours truly on *Extra Big Scoop!* last night? Occasion-
ally I'm called upon to dish over the airwaves because
they know at Wolf Radio News that I've got way too much
dirt to be confined to one weekly column!

Reporter **Janine Jewel** beat me to the Extra Big Scoop!
regarding carmaker heiress **Tiffany Ketteride's** surprise
sonogram (twins!), but I gave her and the television audience an Extra Big Double Scoop! when I revealed that
**Caro Dixon's** got a new way of spending $$$ on dam-
ages! Yes, on a crazed, drunken bender that's taken her
from Miami to Aspen to Hawaii, she has broken glass and
ceramics (but no hearts) and torn up shades, sod, and de-
signer sheets! This one's outta control in a way her fellow
Inheritance Club members can't keep up with!

10:28 a.m. October 24, 20—
To: revbill@reacres.com
From: dfarms@azlinx.com
Subject: Don't know as I have one

Dear Rev,

I'm sure Bev's golf partner is very nice, but remember, I don't golf. Maybe I'll meet her someday, but right now, I just can't leave this little colt. Flipper's as cute as a button and fast as all get-out and responds to my whistle better than the pile of fur who at this moment is using my foot as a pillow. (Poor old Kirby—lucky he twitches when he dreams because that's about the only exercise he gets.)

I heard from both kids yesterday. The village Paul is in is pretty remote, but he sends me an e-mail every time he goes into town. Imagine cybercafés in a place called Bolgatanga! He's doing great; he's got fourteen students altogether, and he says one guy in particular is a mathematical genius. Paul says the kid gets so excited figuring out a problem he actually laughs! Hearing that reminded me of one of your better sermons—the one about enjoying your gifts. (I remember

Cassie taking her compact mirror out of her purse and handing it to me, saying, "Enjoy yours.")

Theresa and her husband are well—Rich is thinking of running for mayor of Anchorage! Theresa says if he wins, he'll give me the keys to the city. I said I'd rather have the keys to a new pickup.

Well, I hear Homer out in the corral—he wants to go for a ride, so I guess I'll go saddle him up.

Cyril

from the desk of
KATHY

*October something*

*Hey Kath—*

*I'm back! I found your scolding little note but I can't seem to find you, so I've wandered into your office. Hope you don't mind me using your stationery.*

*I keep forgetting Hawaii can be a lousy place for a redhead. I got freckled and I hate getting freckled. Where are you anyway?*

*Hey, why didn't you show me these RSVPs? (I'm not snooping— they're right here in a folder on top of your desk.) They're funny! "Mr. Trehorn has other plans." (Yeah, like declaring bankruptcy because his Vegas monopoly's not a monopoly anymore.) "Ms. Ellis remembers what happened at your last party." (She shouldn't—she was passed out the whole time!) "Hank Fischer is otherwise engaged." (Yeah, at making movies no one wants to see.) Well, I'm glad I'm not having a party—who'd want to waste time with these losers anyways?*

*But you should have shown me them, Kathy. What were you try-ing to do, protect me? You're always meddling around in my life, and you know what? I'm sick of it! In fact, why don't you quit meddling and* look for another job. *Because I don't need you protecting me or hunting me down to send me crap or lecturing me, blah blah blah, etc. etc. etc.!*

*Call Ernst to pick up your check.*

*C.*

6:14 a.m.  October 24, 20—
To: mbc@ebpub.com
From: isleast@nsd.com
Subject: Greetings from the ex-Luddite


Dear Meg:

After your annual get-Astrid-off-the-island visit, I always write you a sorry-you-failed-but-didn't-we-have-fun-
anyway note, but this is historic—my first by e-mail! I
had the usual wonderful time with you, and I really appreciate your guidance and technical know-how regarding
the laptop. I can hardly believe my little island's wired and
I am too; while I didn't think this place was immune to
progress, I thought I might be. (Maybe more wary than
immune . . .)

I imagine it will be easier to work with you online; still, I
think I'll print out everything you send me just so I can get
my red pencil out!

Thanks too for the books—that's what I always look forward to, the "surprise" stack of new books. You've done so
well at EB! "Vice president" has such a nice ring to it—of
course we were always the smartest ones there!

Your thoroughly modern friend,

Astrid

P.S. I'm having such fun on the Internet—why, I can even type in "EBPublishing" and I go right to its Web page! Of course, I suppose you know that. . . .

3:37 p.m.  October 25, 20—
To: isleast@nsd.com
From: mbc@ebpub.com
Subject: Re: Greetings from the ex-Luddite

Dear Astrid:

It always is a bit jarring to leave the piney wildness of your lovely island and return to the hullabaloo of London. The view from my office window is quite different than the view from your front room: I look out and see people in front of buildings, while you look out and see the Atlantic behind trees.

Everyone—at least everyone who was here when you were—asked the usual questions: "What's she do out on that island anyway?" "Is she ever coming back to London?" "Why hasn't such a pretty thing married?" (The last was asked by that old lech, Montgomery.)

Actually, I ask myself those same questions. I must admit I'm beginning to worry a bit about you, Astrid. I do think you need to expand your circle of friends—corresponding with companies and authors who've disappointed you does not count as a social life. And as much as I hate to say you're not getting any younger, it's true: *you're not getting any younger.* I don't want you to wind up some crazy hermit, clomping down the path to the shore in your clogs, your blond hair gone white, muttering under your breath.

I think you should come to me for our next vacation. Or perhaps I'll ditch Alex and the kids and the two of us can go off to Spain or Italy on a real holiday.

Love,

Meg

P.S. I've attached a manuscript—please do your magic on it and let me have it back by the beginning of next month.

P.P.S. I showed you how to open an attachment, but if your mind had too much cyberinfo to absorb and you've forgotten . . . look at the manual!

P.P.P.S. Or call me.

from the desk of
KATHY

10/25/20—

Caro—

If you picked up your damn cell phone once in a while, I could have told you this in person. Now I'm leaving this note by the bar because at least I know you'll find it.

I have been an assistant to two TV stars, a TV executive, and a movie star's wife. You were the most fun of all of them *when you were fun,* but like the girl in the poem, *when you were bad you were horrid.*

I just can't take it anymore. I've gone past being afraid for you, being mad at you, and being embarrassed by you. Now I'm just sick of you.

So, having said all that, I'll say this: you can't fire me because I quit. Please, *please* don't contact me. I really don't want to hear from you.

Kathy

From the "Here's Buzz" column in *Star Gazer* magazine, October 30, 20—

Heads were turning as **Senator Geoff Purdy** entered the Watergate Hotel for the annual D.C. No Tricks/All Treat Ball. Starting just five years ago as a small fundraiser for the international relief organization GiveSum, the No Tricks/All Treat Ball has morphed into one of the most glamorous, better-be-seen-at fêtes and officially starts the holiday season of giving for the swank set. But the young senator, looking more handsome than a pol should, also looked more relieved, no doubt happy to have avoided running into heiress **Caro Dixon**. At last year's ball, the dipsomaniac Dixon, when she wasn't waving down the bartenders, found great sport in grabbing the dashing politician by the tails of his tux, crying, "You've got my vote, Purdy-boy!"

There were none of the usual hijinks committed by Miss $$$Bags, because she was not in attendance. Odd, as GiveSum is one of Caro's pet charities . . . odder still is that the rich redhead has been decidedly MIA of late . . . wasn't in attendance at **Blake Brenner's** birthday bash or at **Paige Gem's** fashion show. Should we put out an APB?

9:43 p.m.   October 31, 20—
To: mberg@cal.com
From: lw@wpalms.com
Subject: Happy Halloween


Dear Mitch,

Thanks again for all your e-mails; they mean so much to Sonia. Today when she was told it was Halloween, she said she wanted to dress up as a Russian princess because "I'm really Anastasia, daughter of the czar!" I said I had no idea she was royalty, and she said, "My family's too dumb to notice—except for Mitchie! That's because he's a prince!"

Thought you'd enjoy that.

Lorraine

## TUCK'ER INN
## COMFORT, QUIET, AND
## CONTINENTAL BREAKFAST

*October? November? Who cares?*

*Dear . . . me,*

*Can you help me? Can you just tell me—where am I? What's a Tuck'er Inn? Am I here because I'm tuck'erd out? Is that red stain on my shirt from blood or sangria? What have I done? What do I do now?*

*Help me, Me. Me, Caroline. Help me. Please.*

From the "Here's Buzz" column in *Star Gazer* magazine, November 6, 20—

Salt Lake City was surprised when rap star **Rippy Ratt** showed up asking for an audition with the Mormon Tabernacle Choir. Seems the very blue songsmith (whose lyrics we can't print in a family newspaper) has had a major conversion and wants to give himself to the Lord via the choir, which he says "raises voices for the Salvation Nation."

And where in the world is **Caro Dixon**? The answer is, she could be anywhere in the world . . . a bar in Belarus . . . a tavern in Turkey . . . a saloon in Senegal. For our Miss $$$Bags truly does have the ways and means to bar-hop around the globe . . . The funny thing is, not one international or American bartender has reported having seen her. Strange, as she's on a first-name basis with at least three thousand of them! So where is she? Calls made to friends and acquaintances came up with no answers, although their comments were uniformly similar: "I don't care where that #@*@!%!* is!"

My suspicious hackles are beginning to rise . . . has the liquor-loving lady finally decided to end the affair with the bottle? Stranger things have happened . . . and you know I'll be the first to report them!

6:55 a.m. November 8, 20—
To: mbc@ebpub.com
From: isleast@nsd.com
Subject: Disillusionment


Dear Meg,

Thanks (I guess) for pointing me toward that *Star Gazer* site, although I must say that after reading it, I felt like I needed a bath! I don't know when gossip became as necessary as daily bread to so many Brits and Americans, but it is a diet of empty calories that causes bloat!

If this were the end of the world, would today's "journalists" report it, or would their stories cover what everyone was wearing to the apocalypse?

Shaking my head,

Astrid

9:42 p.m. November 9, 20—
To: revbill@reacres.com
From: dfarms@azlinx.com
Subject: Teeth and Tabloids


Hey Bill,

Strangest thing—I was sitting in my dentist's office (yep, *again*—they put up the Golden Gate bridge faster than this guy can build mine) and couldn't find a *National Geographic* in the whole pile to read. What I did find was not one but *four* magazines with pictures of Caroline Dixon on the cover. You remember me telling you about a girl at the ranch years ago who said, "Is this some kind of cult?" after I'd invited the kids to go to church with Cass and me? Remember, the ambassador to Spain or something's daughter? That was Caroline Dixon.

She was like a high-spirited filly who could turn into either a great champion or a terror, busting out of the stall gate and trampling anyone in her way. Anyway, from all the articles, it looks like she didn't have the right trainer. Poor kid.

Give my love to Bev.
Cyril

From the "Here's Buzz" column in *Star Gazer* magazine, November 13, 20—

Ladies and gents, the case of the Redheaded Guzzler in Gucci has been solved! Sources say that **Caroline Dixon** is finally fed up with sex on the beach—and other specialty drinks! Yes, in an effort to banish future hangovers, Miss $$$Bags finally woke up and heard the very loud music: "You've got a drinking problem! You're a mess!" Sources say she's holed up at one of those fancy dry-out clinic/spas in flyover land, giving "the program" that ol' college try.

How, I wonder, will that affect the voting? After making my announcement last week on *Extra Big Scoop!* that the Most Unadmired Man and Woman of the Year poll was open, names began pouring in (look for the results in our year-end wrap-up issue). So far the name most often poured: Caroline Dixon! But will her rendezvous with rehab earn her sympathy non-votes? Or will remembrances of her past outrageous behavior bring in the votes? Other ignotables who've brought in more than one vote include **Blake Brenner**, actor with an attitude; **Congressman Ralph Lassiter** (is there a cookie jar he *hasn't* stuck his hand in?); evangelist **Hap Humphries,** who wants America to launch a new civil war between Christian states and godless ones; and celebrity dog trainer **Alice Mazlech,** whose excellent training results might have something to do with the tranquilizers she was secretly videotaped stirring into the Puppy Chow.

Looking over the front-runners, I see that they're all worthy candidates, but there are many, many, *many* out there who are as deserving as these to be America's Most Unadmired. . . .

7:32 a.m. November 14, 20—
To: thebuzz@sg.com
From: isleast@nsd.com
Subject: Standards


Dear "Mr. Buzz,"

Years ago I had the fortune of being in the employ of Ambassador Henry Dixon's family, serving as nanny to the then thirteen-year-old Caroline Dixon. Although I was engaged barely a year, I enjoyed my service with them immensely.

For the past ten years I have been living on an island in the Boknafjorden of Norway. I enjoy my seclusion here, and when I don't, I can always get in the boat and go to the mainland. However, my island is not immune to progress, and when it became "wired," I decided to follow suit. I appreciate the ability to read about things unavailable to me through the small island library and my subscription to *Aftenposten*.

In looking up Caroline Dixon, I came across your magazine and specifically your column, and my questions to you are these:

1. What purpose do you serve?
2. Do you consider what you do a waste of talent?
3. Doesn't your conscience bother you?

The Caroline Dixon I knew was a very bright child living under difficult circumstances. Why not, instead of exacerbating problems, try to help solve them?

Sincerely,

Astrid Brevald

P.S. I would never lower myself to vote in your silly poll, but if I did, I might find myself writing your name.

3:14 p.m.  November 14, 20—
To: isleast@nsd.com
From: thebuzz@sg.com
Subject: Re: Standards


Dear Ms. Brevald:

I don't worry about my conscience when I write about spoiled, über-rich young girls who have nothing better to do with their inheritance than drink and spend it away. While I have not met Caro Dixon personally, other colleagues have, and their report is that she treated them rudely.

When a very public person lives a very public life, she cannot pick and choose when she wants attention and when she doesn't.

And please, don't lecture me about wasting my talent. I'm providing a service to readers by writing a humorous column featuring those people they want to read about. Sorry, but I am not responsible for whatever humor genes you may or may not carry.

The Buzz

P.S. Thanks for the vote!

From the "Here's Buzz" column in *Star Gazer* magazine, November 20, 20—

All of Hollywood turned out for the premiere of *Kimchee for Cookie,* the international (made in Bangkok and Tokyo by Korean director **Loh Sung**, starring Italian actor **Benito Fiorucci** and American **Gina Whelvan** in her breakout role) romantic comedy/martial arts pic that's got boffo box office written all over it. About a year ago, at the Can-Can club in NYC, yours truly asked the fresh-faced actress how she felt about snagging the coveted part.

"I couldn't have gotten it without the support of my friends," said the beaming Miss Whelvan, nodding toward heiress **Caro Dixon,** who was balancing a supersized cosmopolitan as she boogied on the dance floor.

This week, yours truly, who's never afraid of the tough questions, asked Miss Whelvan what she thinks about her supportive friend now. "I mean, didn't she cold-cock you in the lobby of the Bangkok Four Seasons?"

"No comment," said the agile actress (she did all her own martial arts stunt work), but the disgusted look on her face spoke volumes.

Sources willing to talk tell me Little Miss Hangover, tucked away in her exclusive dry-out spa, isn't saying much in group sessions but does use her share of tissues. And what exactly is she crying about? The tacky décor of the common room and the low thread count of the bed-sheets?

You'd think, especially in light of the upcoming holi-day, that Miss $$$Bags would realize all she has to be thankful for. There aren't too many of us in her strato-spheric money bracket!

To you, faithful readers, happy Thanksgiving, and re-member, I'll always be here to pass the dish. . . .

8:18 a.m.  November 22, 20—
To: thebuzz@sg.com
From: isleast@nsd.com
Subject: Thankfulness


Dear "Mr. Buzz,"

When you're celebrating your Thanksgiving holiday, do you give thanks for the omniscient powers that allow you to write about what Caroline Dixon is thinking about when she cries? Or are you thankful you don't have any of that bothersome compassion, which might get in the way of your story? Or are you grateful that people are fallible, therefore giving you topics to write about?

Just wondering,

Astrid Brevald

3:05 p.m.  November 22, 20—
To: isleast@nsd.com
From: thebuzz@sg.com
Subject: Re: Thankfulness


Here's what I'm thankful for: a readership of over 2 million people who recognize *satire* when they read it.

No one's asking you to read my column.

The Buzz

7:35 a.m.  November 23, 20—
To: thebuzz@sg.com
From: isleast@nsd.com
Subject: Re: Re: Thankfulness


Dear "Mr. Buzz,"

It's true, English is my second language, but having ma-
jored in it at the University of Oslo and having gotten a further degree at Cambridge, I feel qualified to tell you that
*satire* is not a synonym for *gossip*.

Astrid Brevald

7:55 p.m.  November 26, 20—
To: mberg@cal.com
From: lw@wpalms.com
Subject: Funny story


Hi Mitch,

Sonia *loved* the chocolate turkeys you sent her and was quite the hostess, sharing them with everyone. They caused a commotion, with patients and their families gobbling and giggling. It was a very festive addition to our Thanksgiving meal!

Later that evening, when I said goodnight to her, she reminded me that her grandson was the one who sent "all those chocolate turkeys." Then she said, "Not only did he send them, he plucked them all by hand! My Mitchie thinks of everything!"

Thought you'd like hearing that.

Lorraine Welby

From the "Here's Buzz" column in *Star Gazer* magazine, November 27, 20—

More news on the heiresses-behaving-badly front (is it something in the Evian?) . . . **Tuscany James**, the lucky girl who, along with her sister, **CiCi**, will one day inherit the entire James Hotel chain, loudly booed **Mindy Menard** as the young actress made her stage entrance in the new Broadway musical *Shazam!* New York audiences like to give their actors a chance before voicing their opinions and therefore turned on stick-thin Tuscany (someone force that girl to order from room service— stat!), forcing her to hightail it out of the theater. Maybe she took a subway up to the borough where Bronx cheers are more encouraged? Wait a sec . . . Tuscany—subway? Tuscany—the Bronx? Doubt it.

But while our Miss James disrupted a theatrical performance, the heiress who can teach all others how to really act up disrupted a far more serious gathering. Yes, **Caro Dixon,** holed up in her chic little Château de Sobriety in flyover land, decided that a group meeting needed a little more than heartfelt confessionals and professional counsel, and got in a slugfest with a shy little teacher's aide from Kalamazoo. (Maybe Gina Welvan and the schoolteacher should team up to do battle against the boxing heiress.) My sources say clinic staff had to peel the pugilistic Caro off the terrified teacher, who probably didn't know drying out was so dangerous! Miss Dixon reportedly walked away from the fight flicking her famous red hair, reminding the dazed group members that "no one ever wins a fight with a Dixon." (History alert: Wasn't Henry Dixon, her father, involved in shady business deals that almost cost him the ambassadorship to Portugal?)

Miss $$$Bags had taken a dip in the polling of the Most Unadmired Man and Woman in America; perhaps this recent behavior will put her among the front-runners!

6:47 a.m.  November 28, 20—
To: thebuzz@sg.com
From: isleast@nsd.com
Subject: I am truly speechless


Dear "Mr. Buzz,"

You have truly gone beyond the pale.

Astrid Brevald

4:32 p.m.  November 28, 20—
To: isleast@nsd.com
From: thebuzz@sg.com
Subject: Re: I am truly speechless


I got all excited when I saw your subject heading.

The Buzz

9:58 p.m. November 28, 20—
To: revbill@reacres.com
From: dfarms@azlinx.com
Subject: Gobble gobble


Dear Rev,

Bev'll be happy to hear that I didn't spend Thanksgiving alone. Two—count 'em—two ladies (Jean, who's got that goiter problem, and cross-eyed Marie) from church stopped by with a big turkey dinner, packaged fancy in covered dishes. Course, I felt obliged to invite them to join me, as they'd brought enough food for half the congregation. I've had worse dinners (those K-rations in Vietnam come to mind), but I've sure had better. I sorta resented their forwardness—especially when they went on about how they missed seeing me in services. Yeah, yeah, I know I should be grateful that they were even thinking of me.

Heard from both kids. No turkey for Paul, of course, but Theresa said she made a 23-pounder and invited just as many people over. She said three or four of them she actually liked, and the others were people they hope will donate to Rich's campaign!

Say, have you been reading all that bull crap about Caroline Dixon? I've started reading some of these tabloids (what's next, soap operas?) and man, I haven't seen anyone ganged up on like that since Cassius Clay changed his name to Muhammad Ali.

Cyril

*6:28 a.m.  November 29, 20—*
*To: dfarms@azlinx.com*
*From: revbill@reacres.com*
*Subject: Re: Gobble gobble*


*Dear Cyril:*


*Jean does not have a goiter and Marie isn't cross-eyed. Still, you didn't kick them out, so I have to be grateful for small favors.*

*Keep reaching out, Cy, and remember that Cassie wanted you to keep yourself open.*

*Pax,*

*Bill*

*9:31 p.m. November 30, 20—*

*Dear Astrid:*

*Here's a name out of your past: Caroline Dixon. You were my sixth (and last) nanny for about a year, until my father died, and although it's been years since we've communicated, I've always thought very highly of you.*

*I don't know if you've heard about me and my recent problems— the American and English press seem to think I live a life worthy of lots of ink—but I've become very fond of things served in goblets, shot glasses, steins, and flutes.*

*Oh, they wouldn't like that, the people who helped me; they believe in telling it like it is. So here goes: my name is Caroline and I am an alcoholic. (Yikes!)*

*Months ago I wrote a joke apology letter that was published without my permission (nobody else thought it was very funny and now I don't either). I just completed a treatment program, and in it I came to see the true value of making amends. So I'm writing a real letter of apology to those people I've hurt in my life. (I hired someone to find your address for me—I hope you don't mind.) You were very kind to me at a time when kindness was hard to come by . . . and all I remember is being mean and*

*snotty to you. And yes, I did let the maid take the fall for break-*
*ing your music box. It was me all along.*

*Again, I'm very sorry for the way I treated you, and I'm sorry it's*
*taken this long for me to tell you.*

*Sincerely,*

*Caroline Dixon*

*P.S. Please tell me the cost of the music box and I'll send you a*
*check.*

7:16 a.m.  December 1, 20—
To: caro@dix.org
From: isleast@nsd.com
Subject: Re: An apology


Dear Caroline:

As I live and breathe . . .

You can't know how much you've been on my mind lately;
you see, I've been following your recent trials, and mostly
with chagrin and consternation!

But no matter how sensational the reporting, I remained
confident that you'd find a way to solve your problems.

I am a bit surprised, however, over your apology, for I truly
don't remember you being a mean and snotty girl (well, no
more than the normal teenage-girl mean and snotty). What
I recall was that you were kind and loving but were being
pulled in directions most teenagers could never fathom!

This may surprise you, but my year with you was one that
I cherish. I always thought of you as a special girl, Caroline,
and I wish you all the best in your recovery.

Remembering that strong will of yours, I am certain that you can do it!

I am so glad you've written me!

Rooting for you,

Astrid Brevald

P.S. The music box was made for me by my grandfather and has no monetary value.

P.P.S. Where are you now? Are you in a place where you'll be safe?

*11:07 p.m. November 30, 20—*
*To: dfarms@azlinx.com*
*From: caro@dix.org*
*Subject: An apology*


*Dear Mr. and Mrs. Dale,*

*Long story short: I was booked for a monthlong vacation at your ranch when I was fourteen years old. My dad was dying, but everyone was pretending that he wasn't, and they sent me away because I was lousy at pretending.*

*You might remember me by the tantrums I threw, the horrible things that came out of my mouth, and my fondness for paying the other "dudes" to do my chores.*

*Once I didn't curry my horse after riding her, and instead of yelling at me, you, Mr. Dale, took me back into the stall, calm as can be, and told me I could take out my anger on you or your wife but never a horse, because a horse never does anything to intentionally hurt a person's feelings. And Mrs. Dale, I can't count the number of times you could have yelled at me but chose instead to treat me with kindness.*

*I had just started having fun at your ranch—just celebrated my fourteenth birthday, in fact—when I was called home with the news my father had died.*

*Anyway, I guess a lot of things have made me the person I am today, which is an alcoholic. (Yikes!) I can't apologize to you with the excuse that I was drunk (I didn't really start to drink until I was twenty-one), but I apologize for letting the horses out of the corral that day and all the time and effort it took to get them back. I also apologize for calling you all those names. I can't remember them, but I know they were bad.*

*Very sincerely,*

*Caroline Dixon*

8:15 a.m. December 1, 20—
To: caro@dix.org
From: dfarms@azlinx.com
Subject: Re: An apology


Dear Miss Dixon,

Do you remember "*#!@*&#!* cowboy moron"? Or how about "dumb *!*!#*! yokel"? Or "stupid #*!*%!*! sodbuster"? In all our years of running the ranch, Mrs. Dale and I had never heard anyone—not even the sons and cousins of a big political family from New Jersey—talk the way you did. But I guess we all have our way of dealing with pain.

If I treated you kindly, it was because Mrs. Dale made me. She was the kind of woman who saw only the good in people, and if there wasn't any good to be seen, she said it was her vision that needed adjusting.

She went to her just rewards almost three years ago. Like your dad, it was cancer that got her. I miss her every day and then some.

I had a hand I was about to fire before he went into AA. He was with me 18 years, right up until I closed the ranch, so I know these kinds of problems can be licked. If you put half the effort into cleaning yourself up as you did into thinking of names to call us, you'll do just fine.

Best of luck to you, and apology accepted, and appreciated.

Sincerely,

Cyril Dale

9:32 a.m. December 2, 20—
To: isleast@nsd.com
From: caro@dix.org
Subject: Hello


Dear Astrid:

I have memorized those things you said about me, even though I'm afraid you might have confused me with someone else. Kind, loving? It means the world to me that you recognized those qualities in me—if I had them once, maybe underneath everything I can find them again.

In response to your question, I don't know if there is such a thing as a safe place for me; my job will be to figure out how to keep myself safe no matter where I'm at. For now, I'm holed up (you'll like this—under the name Becky Thatcher!) in the Pierre Hotel in Manhattan. My suite overlooks Central Park, and I like to sit and watch the world go by.

Because of my weird circumstances, meetings are hard to go to, but my sponsor and I talk a lot. Other than that I'm alone, but not really lonesome . . . well, sometimes I am, but I figure I have so much work to do to get to know the real me that I need to sequester myself for a while. Still, I'd love it if you kept writing. I kept the letters you wrote to me after I was sent away to school.

*Forgive me for not writing you back then, but I was just so mad at everything, even your concern. When the letters stopped coming, I felt betrayed, expecting you'd keep writing even without a response from me. The last I heard was that you were with that American family. How did that work out? Where are you now? Do you have kids of your own? Are you 300 pounds from those wonderful cinnamon cookies you used to bake?*

*Looking forward to hearing more,*

*Caroline*

8:34 p.m. December 2, 20—
To: caro@dix.org
From: isleast@nsd.com
Subject: Re: Hello


Dear Caroline,

Because of your age at the time, I spared you the details of
why and how I came to you, but I'd like to share them with
you now and give you an example of the kind and loving
girl you were.

I had been living a life that as a little *barn* in Norway I never
could have imagined. I was your age, twenty-six, when I
began working as an editorial assistant for an esteemed
publishing house in London. There I enjoyed a life of
manuscripts, author meetings, and the company of my colleagues, whose sensibilities aligned with mine. The sensibilities of one colleague in particular *seriously* aligned with
mine, and we fell in love and the whole world was roses, as
it is when you're young and in love. He was an important
editor whose authors not only were beloved by their readers but won prizes by the bucketful, and we had a relation-
ship that was wonderful for five years, until I began
wondering what direction it might be taking and made
such enquiries to him. Byron (sometimes I prefaced his

name with "Lord," an appellation he didn't seem to mind at all!) liked to be in charge of all things, including his life, and did not like it when a naive—or so he thought—Norwegian woman made demands upon him. Silly me—I thought they were just questions.

Still, we hung on for three more challenging years, and I might have continued for thirty more had not a young woman from the Midlands ventured down to London. Hired as his temporary secretary, she swept him off his feet. I was *knocked* off mine; they were married two months after she typed his first memo, and I resigned my position.

It sounds silly now, but I was seriously bereft and had no idea what to do with myself until a former co-worker, an acquaintance of your mother's, told me that the American ambassador to Portugal and his wife were looking for a nanny for their daughter. Although I had never considered the position of nanny, one thing led to another, and after several interviews I took a flight to Lisbon.

I was frightened and intimidated when I walked into the grand residence of the Count of Olivals, met only by a starchy butler and a skinny, redheaded girl.

"Lucky you," you said, sticking out your hand. "I'm your charge."

I'll never forget that—it made me laugh. And then you laughed and asked if I liked American candy, because you had "tons of it."

By that afternoon you had made me a fan of Kit Kats, Mars bars, and Fireballs. You'd also made me a fan of yours.

More later, I've got to catch a ferry.

*Vennlig hilsen,*

Astrid

8:01 p.m.  December 3, 20—
To: mberg@cal.com
From: lw@wpalms.com
Subject: Another "Sonia-ism"


Hi Mitch—

Today while sitting in the decorated dayroom, your grand-mother informed us that she invented the Christmas tree. Your parents, who were visiting, laughed, and your mother, who has learned it doesn't hurt to play along, said, "Tell us about it."

"Well," said Sonia, "I had just discovered the theory of rela-tivity, and I thought I needed a break from such deep think-ing. So I decided to think of something not so consequential, something fun. So then I thought, what about dressing trees up in jewels, the way fancy ladies dress up to go out?"

Thought you'd enjoy that.

Lorraine

From the "Here's Buzz" column in *Star Gazer* magazine, December 4, 20—

Big doings in London, as British heiress **Penny Englehart** threw a party to announce her engagement to **Dennis Cheltham**, whose new play, *Hostage to America,* is *the* hot ticket on the West End. All of Britan's royalty—inherited and earned—was there, including **Gillian Hedges**, half sister of formerly (?) half-tanked heiress **Caroline Dixon.** But among the swills, there lurked no redhead demanding refills at the bar, no redhead staggering on the dance floor, no redhead picking fights or flashing photographers. Oh, Miss $$$Bags—wherefore art thou? We miss you and your antics—antics readers haven't forgotten, apparently, as you're still the number one vote collector in *Star Gazer's* Most Unadmired Man and Woman in America poll.

Gillian, older by seven years than Caroline and poorer by *millions,* was tight-lipped when asked about the whereabouts of her li'l seester.

I thought she might stay holed up near the treatment facility and its support staff, but then I thought, no, Caroline Dixon wouldn't stay willingly in a part of the country that considers crushed potato chips a worthy au gratin to casseroles. So scouts, keep your eyes open for a desperate redhead looking for a drink . . . of water?!

*10:00 p.m.  December 4, 20—*
*To: dfarms@azlinx.com*
*From: caro@dix.org*
*Subject: Hello*


*Hello Mr. Dale,*

*Other than my former nanny's, yours is the only response I've gotten to my letters and e-mails. (I don't write that to sound petty—I don't know if I'd write me back either! I just want you to know how much I appreciated it.) I also wanted to let you know that I'm sorry about your wife.*

*I remember after one particularly hard day (I don't think there was anyone left on that ranch I hadn't alienated—including the horses), she knocked on our bunkhouse door and came in to tell us there was a campfire with marshmallows waiting for us by the creek. Well, the three other "cowgirls" couldn't get out of there fast enough, but I stayed in my bunk, curled up and staring at the rough planked wall. I don't know if I could have felt any sorrier for myself. Then all of a sudden I heard a few guitar chords and Mrs. Dale started singing. It was a simple, catchy song about a horse, and it didn't take long before I was singing along with it—in my head, because I didn't want to give her the satisfaction of cheering me up. So I just lay there, facing the* wall. She kept singing, though, and then she pretended she forgot a word.

"First you gotta have a horse, have a horse, have a horse,
And a pair of shiny—"

She kept playing that verse over and over, as if she'd forgotten the word boots and wanted me to prompt her. It was driving me crazy, and finally I flipped over in my bunk and yelled, "Boobs!"

There was silence for a few moments, and I thought, "Well, now, I'm gonna get it," but then she started laughing, and I was so surprised at her laughter that I started laughing, and she started playing the song again, and we wound up singing a bunch of different versions, changing the words—"First you gotta have a hearse, and a pair of shiny stiffs"—laughing like crazy

I don't know how long we sang for, but she was so unrushed and easygoing it seemed like forever. I eventually went out to the campfire and wound up having a good (surprise!) time.

She sure was a nice lady.

Caroline

10:14 p.m. December 4, 20—
To: caro@dix.org
From: dfarms@azlinx.com
Subject: Re: Hello


She *was* a nice lady. It surprised me when God took her, because it was so clear that she could do so much more good work right here. It's not like the world is overrun with good people doing good things.

I just got in from sitting in front of the fire pit. Twenty-two years of running the dude ranch × approx. 300 clients a year = a lot of campfires. Plus me and Cassie would often as not end the day in front of one—especially after the kids left home—with her playing guitar and singing and me and the dog staring at her like she was the gol-darnedest greatest thing ever. Kirby's tongue was always hanging out, probably mine too.

We used to joke, me and Cassie, that together we made the perfect cowboy. We both were born on farms—her on a big cattle ranch in North Dakota and me on a smaller one in Montana—and she could ride as good as me. I was a better roper, but she was a better herder. I was stronger, but she was smarter.

We both could cook—do you remember our famous chili and corn bread? She could play guitar and sing, and I could listen.

I used to thank the Lord every day for my Cassie. Now that she's gone, I ask Him every day, "Why?" Can't say as I've heard an answer.

Tonight, the sky was big and black and the stars were doing their starry business. It's a comfort to sit under a sky like that with a fire popping and throwing sparks. I used to sit there with Cassie's guitar propped up against a rock, and sometimes I could swear I heard the wind vibrate the strings. I'd pretend it was Cassie, saying hello.

Whew! I think the best place for me right now is bed, instead of sitting in front of this glowing computer screen sounding some kind of crazy.

Cyril

P.S. When you were here at the ranch, I spoke to your nanny a couple times—I remember she sounded like a Swedish television actress.

P.S.S. You sound good. I'm proud of you.

7:44 a.m.  December 5, 20—
To: thebuzz@sg.com
From: isleast@nsd.com
Subject: Your inanity, again


Dear "Mr. Buzz,"

Just when I think you can't sink any lower, you fall another mile!

Why can't you leave Caroline Dixon in peace? Can't you understand she's trying to rebuild a life you helped knock down?

Out of everyone in the world, isn't there someone else you can throw your considerable scorn at?

Astrid Brevald

4:17 p.m.  December 5, 20—
To: isleast@nsd.com
From: thebuzz@sg.com
Subject: Re: Your inanity, again


Dear Ms. Brevald:

I can't leave Caroline Dixon alone because she's good copy.
Got that? People like to read about her, and the more I write
what people like to read, the more they buy the magazine and
the more money I get paid. Got it? It's a simple tenet of capi-
talism: give the people what they want.

And again, I would suggest to you, if you don't like it, don't
read it.

The Buzz

*8:10 a.m. December 5, 20—*
*To: isleast@nsd.com*
*From: caro@dix.org*
*Subject: It's me*


*Good morning, Astrid:*

*Do you know what an odd thing it is to be up and about at 8:00 in the morning? I've already read half the paper and had a very healthy breakfast of oatmeal and tomato juice. Then I had an unhealthy caramel roll.*

*There are a few sprinkles of snow but they seem pretty tentative, as if they haven't been invited to stick around yet. I'm going out to encourage them after I finish writing my faithful correspondents. (You and the cowboy make me excited to check my e-mail!) I take a big long walk every day and one of the beauties of winter is that I bundle myself up and people don't recognize me! The staff here is very discreet, and so far there have been no paparazzi at the doors. I FEEL STRANGELY NORMAL!*

*I was thinking about addiction last night (I still have trouble getting to sleep—anytime I lie down, my brain all of a sudden turns into a carnival, with all the rides going at once), realizing that it wasn't the alcohol I was most addicted to but the attention. The alcohol was a lubricant for the machinery that allowed* me to get that attention, oiling those old inhibitions so that I could act crazy. I think I'm perfectly capable of having a good time without alcohol; what I'm worried about is whether I can have a good time without the attention.

But right now I don't need anything but this good coffee and the park view and the knowledge that you will write me back. I like that knowledge, Astrid.

Caroline

P.S. I remember you telling me about your family's island. You made it sound sort of boring—what made you go back there?

*8:33 a.m.  December 5, 20—*
*To: dfarms@azlinx.com*
*From: caro@dix.org*
*Subject: It's me*


*Good morning, Cyril:*

*Did you know I've known three other Cyrils in my life? One was the butler in the country house of my friend Penny, one was a boy who wore his school tie even when he was on vacation, and one was a bass player in the punk band EAT. The name suited all three of them, even though they were all very different from one another, but for some reason, Cyril doesn't seem to fit a cowboy. No offense, of course.*

*I liked when you told me about Mrs. Dale. I've always believed there were special marriages out there; I'd just never seen any up close and personal. My own parents fought for a long time, and then they stopped, and the fighting almost seemed better than the cease-fire because they were always so tense then; no matter if the flooring was carpet or tile or wood, it was always as if we were walking on eggshells. (Sorry, sometimes too much coffee gets in the way of my descriptive powers.)*

*You probably have heard about my father, Henry Dixon—I adored him, and I think the feeling was mutual, but he was*

hardly ever around for me to really test that theory. It's funny—
I remember him home fighting or not fighting with my mother,
but I don't remember him home doing much of anything with me.

My mother's the English one, pretty and pink-cheeked and definitely proud to be a lady. Definitely the sort of mother who liked
to see her children on a limited schedule, as long as the children
(my sister and I) were clean and polite and didn't demand too
much in the way of attention.

I hesitate to send this, Cyril—I don't like how I sound—but my
sponsor tells me I should never be afraid to be honest.

So there you have it, a little honesty amid the boo-hooing.

Caroline

P.S. I don't know when the last time was that someone said they
were proud of me!

10:30 p.m. December 5, 20—
To: caro@dix.org
From: dfarms@azlinx.com
Subject: Re: It's me


Dear Caroline:

Well, here, I'll say it again: I'm proud of you. There,
now you know *exactly* the last time someone told you
that.

I had this morning what I hope is my last visit to my
dentist. If he charged by the hour, he'd be a billionaire;
the guy is the slowest man on earth and has been tin-
kering with my teeth for what seems an eternity.

Maybe it's the new receptionist's influence (she's
about thirty years younger than the old one), but now
there are tabloids and weeklies in the waiting room,
and because Dr. Slo-Mo is slow with everyone, you do
a lot of waiting in his office. Anyway, that's my long-
winded excuse for telling you I've been reading about
you in junk I normally wouldn't pick up. That's another
reason why I'm proud of you—I don't know how anyone could put up with that kind of junk. Stalkers with

cameras and notebooks . . . I've got a couple old branding irons I'd like to use on them.

There's a real estate agent in town who drives out here every couple months to see if I want to put the ranch up for sale. She's fond of that popular phrase "You've got to move on" and thinks I should. "Could my moving on have anything to do with your big fat commission?" I finally asked. That shut her proverbial yap, but just wait, come February she'll be out here again.

Nippy here tonight. I've got the fireplace going and a pot of decaf going. Still like the flavor, but the caffeine's murder.

Your friend,

Cyril

6:17 a.m.  December 6, 20—
To: caro@dix.org
From: isleast@nsd.com
Subject: Re: It's me


Dear Caro:

It's a treat to go to my inbox these days! And you sound so well! That is what makes me so happy, Caroline, and what makes me marvel too! (Look at me, three exclamation points in a row—as an editor, I never allow my writers to do that, but now I find myself in need of an editor, having grown windier and windier as time marches on. . . .)

What impresses me the most is your commitment to pick yourself up, despite those who would love nothing more than to see you trip. I'm talking about the press, of course, and specifically that awful columnist who writes "The Buzz" in that awful paper, *Star Gazer.* How do you stand it?

I'm sorry; I just get so angry at the lies that are printed about you. I still shudder to think of my own brief experience with vultures masquerading as photographers; my admiration of your forbearance in handling those armed with cameras or pens is deep.

*Vennlig hilsen,*
Astrid

*5:18 p.m. December 6, 20—*
*To: isleast@nsd.com; dfarms@azlinx.com*
*From: caro@dix.org*
*Subject: You two*

*Dear Astrid and Cyril,*

*I hope you don't mind that I'm sending you the same e-mail, but it was so funny that you both wrote me about the press that I'm going to economize on cyberspace rather than saying the same thing twice. Besides, I think you two should meet, seeing as you both knew me around the same time. So, Astrid, meet Cyril; Cyril, may I present Astrid.*

*Thinking has been my favorite pastime of late, about everything and everyone, including the press. For historical perspective, let's go back . . . back in time . . .*

*Both of you know, to varying extents, of my father, Henry Dixon. His was a Horatio Alger story: a poor kid raised by a single mother in Gilroy, California, who with a lot of smarts and hard work (and a lifelong distaste of garlic) got a scholarship to UCLA, graduated with a degree in economics, then went to Stanford for an MBA. The usual combination of ambition and luck landed him work in the manufacturing company (crates, I think it was) of his roommate's father. More ambition, more luck, and eventually he bought out his roommate, then his roommate's father, after which he bought more and more companies in the United States and around the world. Everything kept building exponentially—his money, his prestige in the business world—and finally, after settling down with his "English rose" and having me, he was appointed ambassador to Portugal.*

*Of course, that's too tame now for readers who want to know where the intrigue is, the payoffs, the sex with high-priced call girls? Fortunately (for the press), a scandal involving government payoffs and "accounting discrepancies" developed, and even though my father was cleared of all charges, there were those who called for him to give up his ambassadorship. Astrid, I'm sure you remember a certain level of tension in the household? Then he suddenly got sick . . . and then he died.*

*I had the first experience of being blinded by flashbulbs when I was called back from your ranch, Cyril, to our London home. I had just turned fourteen years old (do you remember? Cassie baked me a cake) and my father had just died and a horde of photographers surrounded me as I got out of the car. Astrid, I'll never forget how you held me close to you, trying to shield my face with your bag. I remember my face was pressed against your chest and I could hear how fast your heart was beating.*

Outside the church too, the photographers' artillery—really, it was like a war, the flashbulbs going off like little bombs—made the whole funeral seem like a movie premiere or the Academy Awards. I couldn't articulate it then, but now I realize how much they trivialized it, what a spectacle it was turned into. I remember holding your hand through the whole service, Astrid, but I don't remember a word that was said, so afraid was I of the regiment of photographers camped outside and ready to fire as soon as the church doors were opened.

Shortly after the funeral, I was sent away to school in Switzerland and sequestered from the press by the school's formidable ivy walls as well as the reporters' disinterest. After all, the big story—my father's death—was over and I was just a skinny redheaded teenager.

The first year was hard. I was mourning a father I loved but didn't know very well, and I was lonesome for you, Astrid. But as I told you, I was so mad and confused, I never responded to your many letters, wouldn't take your calls. Imagine if I had and you had been in my life, in my corner, all these years!

I wasn't emotionally ready to invest in friendships, but I enjoyed the schoolwork—I always enjoyed the schoolwork! (I did hear from the headmistress once, after one particularly notorious tabloid appearance in which I was drunk and trying to French-kiss a member of the British Parliament. "Why, Caroline, you were class valedictorian! You were the lead scorer of the lacrosse team and editor of the school paper! We had expectations of you running the world!")

Wanting to somehow pay homage to my dad and my American half, I went to UCLA for two and a half years, enjoying my studies immensely. It was still hard for me to make friends, but at least I was trying. Then I turned twenty-one and my mother contested my inheritance and the world was suddenly very interested in "the Junior Mint." (The tongue-twister, "the Rich Witch of Westwood" was another favorite.) I couldn't walk across campus without some photographer jumping out of the bushes, and my teachers and the friends I'd started to make began treating me differently . . . so I dropped out. Dropped out of school and into the party scene because I didn't know what else to do.

This is the strange thing about celebrity: as bothersome and sometimes frightening as it is, you start to get used to photographers documenting every latte you buy at Starbucks, you get used to seeing your name in boldface. And the emptier you start to feel—because you know you're really not worth the attention; after all, my celebrity had nothing to do with any of my talents or achievements—the more you want to see those pictures of you buying your latte, the more you want to read your name in boldface, because they help you fool yourself that you matter.

*And then to make sure the attention doesn't go away, you decide to give the press some things to write about, and the more outrageous you are, the more you're written about and the more you're photographed. And the alcohol fuels the behavior that attracts the story, and on and on . . .*

*I'm not excusing the paparazzi because they've gotten predatory and spit at the idea of privacy, but I'm not excusing myself either. If blame were laid, 50 percent of it would go to them and 50 percent to me.*

*Hello—anyone still awake?*

*Caro*

*P.S. I hope that part about the French kissing didn't offend you, Cyril.*

7:44 p.m. December 6, 20—
To: caro@dix.org; isleast@nds.com
From: dfarms@azlinx.com
Subject: Re: You two

You didn't offend me, Caroline. I have French-kissed before, you know. I get the impression that you think I'm an old man, which is understandable, I guess. I probably seemed old the last time you saw me. I'm only fifty-nine, though, and believe it or not, some people consider that young.

I took a ride after I got your e-mail. Just me and Homer and the red mesas and the blue sky. It's something I enjoy so much, that time on my horse with whatever thought I care to think and the quiet to think it in. But your story made me jumpy. What if a guy with a camera leaped up from behind the brush, snapping my picture? Then another, and another?

I get mad just thinking about it, about my peace of mind and my right to be alone being so disrespected. I get mad thinking about how that intrusion—only it's more than an intrusion—is a part of your daily life. To tell you the truth, I'm surprised you're not in the loony bin.

If I could, I'd take my rope and lasso anyone who tried to take your picture. Then I'd toss him into the bull's pen and see how he likes getting charged.

Your friend,

Cyril

6:35 a.m.  December 7, 20—
To: caro@dix.org; dfarms@azlinx.com
From: isleast@nds.com
Subject: Re: You two

(Dear Cyril—Did you intend to reply to me too? If not, sorry; but it's too late, I already read it. I don't know if you remember, but we spoke several times while Caroline was staying at your ranch. I'm the other person to whom Caroline sent her e-mail.)

Dear Caroline *and* Cyril (as long as you're already here, you can read this too)—

The paparazzi problem is not 50 percent your fault. In fact, I don't know if you're at fault at all, because think of it— who among us hasn't done stupid things? The memories are enough to cringe at; imagine if we had a photo documenting the night we drank too much, or yelled at someone, or picked our nose in the car. I think, too, that the documentation amplifies the misdeed, and I'll bet when it comes to publication, the worst picture on the proof sheet is chosen!

I hope you don't mind, Caroline, but I've exchanged a few heated e-mails with one of the worst offenders in the gossip trade—"Mr. Buzz." The things he writes in his columns are so ridiculous, so mean-spirited; well, I just couldn't keep silent. That man needs to be dressed down but good.

It's snowed all day here and my cross-country skis are leaning next to the back door, ready and waiting.

*Vennlig hilsen,*

Astrid

P.S. Really, Caroline, fifty-nine's not so old.

*11:07 a.m. December 7, 20—*
*To: isleast@nsd.com*
*From: caro@dix.org*
*Subject: Audacious Astrid*

*Dear Astrid,*

*I'm touched that you told "Mr. Buzz" to buzz off! Thanks for sticking up for me!*

*I used to read him for laughs, but then it just got too dispiriting—he really does seem to have something against me. Even at the clinic, I managed to hear about the nasty things he was writing: a patient's sister gave him a copy of* Star Gazer *and he gave it to me, as if he were giving me a present. It didn't matter that I was accused of being in a nonexistent fight. This guy was so excited: "Look, you're all over the place!" (My sponsor reminds me that people wouldn't get so excited over false validation if they didn't have so much trouble validating themselves.)*

*It's snowing here too, a little more assertively than the other day. It's whitening up the park, and I just saw some tourists wearing twin Green Bay Packers jackets standing with their heads tipped back, catching snowflakes in their mouths. Then they grabbed each other and kissed with a passion that surprised me. I was taken aback, and I thought, "Am I that much of a snob that passion from some Wisconsin football fans surprises me? Where do I get off?"*

*I didn't used to be like that, did I? I struggle so much with the Caroline I think I really am and the Caroline I thought I've had to be.*

*Any Nordic wisdom on this?*

*Caro*

7:09 a.m. December 8, 20—
To: caro@dix.org
From: isleast@nsd.com
Subject: Re: Audacious Astrid

*Kjaer* Caroline,

My "Nordic wisdom" tells me you're doing just fine. Better than fine.

Before I left for Portugal, I ran into a friend of the man who had thrown me aside for his temp secretary. This gentleman was also an editor at the publishing house and treated all women there as though they were children.

"Tell me, Astrid, how are you qualified to be a nanny? You've spent your young womanhood consumed with nothing but Byron and books!"

At first I smiled; it was in my nature to give people the benefit of the doubt. But this time sanity bested politesse and I realized there was no doubt here!

"Well, it's more a companion position," I said, before adding, "Now tell me, Clive, how are you qualified to be anything but a pompous ass?"

I tell you this story for two reasons, Caroline. One, I think of how you can't even have the pleasure of telling someone off without having it reported on, and two, you really were a companion. Remember the hours and hours we spent reading aloud to each other on the beach at Faro? *Huck Finn* and *A Tale of Two Cities, Sense and Sensibility,* and *The Great Gatsby?* What bliss to lie under a gorgeous yellow sun and pass those books back and forth as the waters of the Costa do Algarve slapped to shore just meters away. It felt as if you and I were alone on that raft with Huck and Tom, or holed up with the Dashwood sisters wondering what had gotten into Willoughby, or sitting out on Gatsby's lawn in our white summer dresses. And oh, the discussions that followed! Your questions and comments could startle me with their depth and maturity; it was as if I were having a conversation with one of my colleagues in the publishing house! I'd look at your little freckled face, your nose peeling from the sun, to remind myself that you were just a girl. You were so curious about everything around you, precocious but never in an aren't-I-smart way.

Oh—my timer's gone off. I gave myself ten minutes to write, and now I must tackle the chores of the day, which include baking several batches of your favorite cinnamon cookies, which are also the favorite of my postman. He complains about his weight gain during the holiday season but says, as far as my cookies go, the extra weight is worth it. Maybe I'll send a batch to your hotel. . . .

*Vennlig hilsen,*

Astrid

10:47 p.m. December 8, 20—
To: isleast@nsd.com
From: dfarms@azlinx.com
Subject: Reacquaintance


Dear Astrid,

I get Christmas cards and the occasional wedding or birth announcement from some of the kids who spent time on the ranch. It's always fun to hear that a kid who cried the first time he got on a horse is now a firefighter or that another kid who always volunteered for KP duty is working as a fancy sous chef. Nobody's e-mailed me like Caroline has, though, and it's a real kick to be in contact with her again. She seems to be doing well, don't you think? It's got to be tough—I hope she's not putting on a brave front for our bene-fit.

So you've been giving that Buzz creep the what-for, eh? Good for you. My wife was a great one for writing to the paper and letting them know what she thought of a new zoning law or water treatment plant. She was a very loving person but wouldn't let people off the hook if she thought a little foot-dangling might be good for them.

I have vivid memories of speaking to you on the phone about Caroline because I thought you sounded just like Inger Stevens on *The Farmer's Daughter* (an old TV show). We don't get many Swedish accents around here.

And I also wanted to tell you I got a laugh out of thinking about the things I've done in just the past twenty-four hours that I'd sure never want to see recorded or photographed for all the world to see.

Anyway, it's nice to meet you—again.

Sincerely,

Cyril Dale

P.S. Does your e-mail address have anything to do with where you live?

3:23 p.m. December 9, 20—
To: dfarms@azlinx.com
From: isleast@nsd.com
Subject: Re: Reaquaintance

Dear Cyril,

Very sharp regarding my e-mail address—I live on an island off the southern coast of Norway. You see, I'm Norwegian, not Swedish. *You* might not think there's much
difference between the two, but believe me, *we* do.

Obviously, I know you're still on your ranch; I gathered
from your use of the past tense when talking of your wife
that she died. If that is not the case, I apologize, and I'll hit
myself for not checking with Caroline first. (While I enjoy
the speed of e-mail, I also recognize a certain carelessness
that comes with it.)

I *think* Caroline's doing all right. From what I've read, her
recovery is a day-to-day process, so I've decided to save my
worry about what may come tomorrow and concentrate on
where she is right now.

I want to tell you a little about the thirteen-year-old girl I
knew because she is a lot different from the thirteen-year-

old girl you knew. She was funny, cheerful, and *so* smart, but the quality I remember most about her was her optimism. She tried and tried to be a good daughter, a good sister, but her efforts were met with a disinterest that, frankly, shocked me. I do think Mr. Dixon truly loved her (and oh, how she loved him!), but he was gone so much of the time that it's hard for a child not to take those absences personally. When he was home it was almost as if she had to make an appointment to see him. As Caroline mentioned, there was a financial scandal that threatened Mr. Dixon's ambassadorship, but even after it was cleared up, the tension remained. It was a family of closed doors, but Caroline kept trying, kept trying, *kept trying* to open them. And always cheerfully, with great heart, as if *this* was going to be the time they'd swing wide open. She was a teenager, but still, when her mother excluded her from dates she made with her elder daughter or her father hunkered down with his lawyers or had to stay another night in another foreign capital, she'd climb into my lap, wrap her arms around my neck, and cry.

When her father got sick, he tried to hide it, and everyone tacitly agreed to act in the charade except for Caroline.

"Daddy, what's the matter?" she asked, her constant question. His constant response was to ignore the question. I know it was a defense mechanism, but I thought it unspeakably cruel not to admit to anyone how sick he was when it was so evident. She started acting out—screaming, cursing, throwing anything that might break—to get some sort of reaction. Their reaction was to send her to your ranch. Everyone knew Mr. Dixon's end was near; they sent her away knowing full well that, barring a miracle, she was never going to see her father again.

I tried—hard, I thought—to stay in her life, but I should have tried harder. I'm going to try as hard as I can to know the woman Caroline is now.

Astrid

From the "Here's Buzz" column in *Star Gazer* magazine, December 11, 20—

So what do you want for Christmas this year? **Hap Humphries**, the fundamentalist firebrand who wants states like California and New York to cede from his "Christian nation," was seen at Bulgari treating himself to a pair of cuff links so studded with diamonds that he's going to need a hoist to lift his arms in prayer. Asked by another customer if the preacher wasn't practicing the sin of greed or at least hubris, Hap recited the always convenient biblical injunction "Judge not lest ye be judged."

And as far as judging, dear reader, your votes for the Most Unadmired Man and Woman in America continue to cause the mailroom grief, coming in as they are by the sackful! Hap, your $74,000 purchase might earn you more points—not that you need them!

And you haven't forgotten the formerly hidden heiress, **Caro Dixon**. Just because she's been out of sight doesn't mean she's out of mind; a large portion of voters have voiced their opinion that Miss $$$Bags is still not-so-admirable.

But back to the qualifier—*formerly* before *missing*. Yes indeedy, while the cantankerous Caro may still be trying to hide from our cameras, she's been found! That's her on the cover, bundled up in swaddling clothes and strolling through danger (well, Fifth Avenue during lunch hour). With the hat, the scarf, and the bulbous down jacket, she'd like us to pretend it's not her, but check out the auburn hair and the pert little nose upon which her signature sunglasses rest. Sources say she's holed up at the Pierre Hotel, living the life of a retired nun. Why retired? Well, she saw the light, and we hope she's lost her habit (glug glug) for good. . . .

7:27 a.m.  December 13, 20—
To: thebuzz@sg.com
From: isleast@nsd.com
Subject: You've really gone too far

There is no salutation because you don't deserve it. How is it you're not in prison, serving out a sentence for the crime of making people's lives unbearable? Shame, shame, shame on you. Caroline Dixon was finally experiencing a little bit of the normalcy the rest of us experience every day, but that was a little bit too much for you and your jackals (yes, I consider you the alpha dog of that pack). No, can't have "Miss $$$Bags" quietly and anonymously enjoying her days, not bothering anyone, because . . . and that's the big question, because why?

I seriously want to know.

Astrid Brevald

10:05 a.m.  December 14, 20—
To: isleast@nsd.com
From: thebuzz@sg.com
Subject: Re: You've really gone too far

I'm not the one who tracked Caroline Dixon down; a photographer found her and sold her picture to our paper. I merely supplied the copy in my signature entertaining way.

I get a lot of e-mail, every day, and let me tell you, it is usually one of two things: praise for what I do or a tip. The number of complaints I get is comparatively infinitesimal, written by the occasional odd duck, of which you are a flock member. Oh, no, wait a second: you are *alpha duck*.

My polite reminder: if you don't like what I write, don't read it.

11:19 p.m.  December 13, 20—
To: thebuzz@sg.com
From: dfarms@azlinx.com
Subject: Caroline Dixon


Dear Mr. Buzz,

You asked in your latest column what people wanted for Christmas. There's only one thing on my list, and that, Mr. Buzz, is to buzzt your jaw. Or maybe your fingers so you can't write anymore. And if you try to sue me for making a threat, I'll sue you back for all the defamatory things you say about Caroline Dixon. Let's just see who wins.

You know how a lot of people say, "Oh, I just don't know what to get so-and-so for Christmas"? Well, I sure would have no trouble getting you the perfect present, and that, Mr. Buzz, would be a *heart.*

Cyril Dale

10:14 a.m.  December 14, 20—
To: dfarms@azlinx.com
From: thebuzz@sg.com
Subject: Re: Caroline Dixon


Dear Mr. Dale:

While I could take action against your threat to "buzzt" (clever) my jaw, in the spirit of the holidays, I'm willing to let it slide. And FYI, just because I might celebrate the *spirit* of the holidays, I don't celebrate Christmas, so there will be no need to get me a present. Besides, what would I do with a heart?

The Buzz

3:03 p.m. December 14, 20—
To: mberg@cal.com
From: lw@wpalms.com
Subject: Sonia

Hello Mitch,

Today Sonia was in her room, throwing all her unmention-ables out of her top dresser drawer. When I asked her what she was doing, she said, "I need more room for all my trea-sures." "What do you mean?" I asked her, and she said, "Mitchie's letters. I need more room for Mitchie's letters." (She saves every e-mail of yours I print out.) I asked her what she planned on doing with all her underwear. "Well, I'm going to donate them to Marilyn Monroe because we wear the same size!"

I get such a kick out of her.

Lorraine

*4:10 p.m. December 14, 20—*
*To: isleast@nsd.com; dfarms@azlinx.com*
*From: caro@dix.org*
*Subject: Found and lost*


*Dear Astrid and Cyril,*

*Another joint e-mail, I don't have the energy to write you separately.*

*Well, my much-enjoyed privacy is no longer . . . man, they are better than bloodhounds at sniffing out their prey. My winter wear was doing the trick, and I was having so much fun being unrecognized and NORMAL, taking long walks through Central Park, sitting and reading in libraries and coffee shops, visiting MOMA and the Guggenheim; I even went skating at Rockefeller Center! What a concept—to be by myself, unbothered, as I think things through. Not lonely, just alone. Astrid, I was such good company to myself!*

*A little horde of photographers has gathered outside across the street, so I can't even look out the window and watch the tourists and the dog walkers and the horse-drawn cabs go by. I'm feeling trapped again, and scared where that feeling will take me. I have been calling my sponsor on the hour.*

*A part of me says, "Stay right where you are—you can't let them win!" (I hate to give up the romantic idea of spending Christmas in New York), and another part tells me to go back to California—at least my house has a big fence. . . .*

*Having my picture taken brought back my pretreatment misery, and I remembered that terribly icky feeling of wanting to taunt them, "How's this for a picture?" and at the same time feeling shame: what did I do to deserve all this attention? That has been what I've been thinking about a lot lately: what do I want to be doing now that I'm sober enough to do something? And I have a thousand answers, and then no answers.*

*Right now I feel so jittery, like I've been mainlining espresso, and that good Christmas vibe I'd been feeling is no more. There's a beautiful sparkly snow that fell, but I can't walk through that winter wonderland. I can't smell those roasting chestnuts, Jack Frost will not be nipping at my nose, and I am seriously doubting the whole peace-on-earth-goodwill-toward-man thing.*

*I know these people eventually will lose interest in me, but what I need to know now is: when?*

*Caro*

9:45 p.m. December 14, 20—
To: dfarms@azlinx.com
From: isleast@nsd.com
Subject: Caroline


Dear Cyril,

After reading Caroline's last e-mail, I was so worried I called her at the hotel. The operator wasn't going to connect me until I remember she's using an assumed name. When I asked for Beeley Thatcher I was put right through.

Cyril, when she heard my voice and I heard hers, both of us broke down and had to spend the first few minutes of our conversation stopping to blow our noses. Her voice (after the crying stopped) sounded just like her voice when she was thirteen—clear and confident, albeit a little more grown-up. I was delighted to hear that voice on so many levels, a prime one being that she didn't sound depressed at all. When I told her this, she laughed (the same wonderful, snorting, slightly indelicate laugh she had when she was younger) and said she had been "in a funk" when she wrote the e-mail.

"But Astrid," she said, "hearing your voice, I'm absolutely schnizzleboggled."

We didn't have our own secret language when we were together, but we did have a few words we'd made up to express certain things: *schnizzleboggled* meant "to be delighted to the nth degree," and we used to say it in our archest British accents.

"What do you say we have a picnic at the beach tomorrow?"

"Oh, darling, I'd be positively schnizzleboggled."

I pride myself on my memory, but I had forgotten that word, and hearing it again just about did me in.

We talked for over an hour and would have talked longer, but she had another call coming in from her sponsor and I didn't want her to miss that.

She doesn't really know what she's going to do next, and although I was cheered at her good mood, I know how fleeting good moods can be.

Astrid

P.S. Another word she reminded me of was *floopin,* which meant "something nasty" (and was usually said in a sweet voice to the short-tempered Austrian cook: "Oh, Anna, that spinach casserole was really floopin"). Then I remembered *greezan*, which she used to describe especially cute teenage boys and I used whenever the attaché to the ambassador dropped by. Oh my, was he *greezan*.

9:07 a.m.  December 15, 20—
To: isleast@nsd.com
From: dfarms@azlinx.com
Subject: What do you think?


Dear Astrid:

I stole two good ideas from you. (1) I've been writing that SOB at *Star Gazer* (in his favor, he wrote me back, but not in his favor is what he wrote). (2) I called up Caroline. I wanted to hear her voice and see if there was anything else I could do to help.

Same here, Astrid—I think she sounded pretty good. But I know whenever my kids call—even if I'm feeling low—I sound pretty good just so they won't worry. So I'm worried about her sounding better than she is.

The last time I saw Caroline was when I drove her to the airport after you called to tell her that her father had died. Astrid, that kid sat there like a rock, only it was like a rock on top of a volcanic mountain. Her whole body was vibrating, and I could see her straining to contain that force that wanted to blow. I tried to comfort her, but she'd say through clenched teeth, "Don't talk!" so I drove on, jabbing the buttons on the radio, hoping to find some magical song or funny DJ that would make her feel better. I was surprised that she let me take her hand in the parking lot, and more surprised when it seemed she wasn't going to let it go—not in the ticket line, not at the gate. She didn't talk, only held my hand, trembling. When they boarded the plane, she kept stalling, kept sitting there despite my telling her, "Come on honey, you've got to go." Finally I sort of dragged her to the gate, practically pushing her into the arms of the ticket agent. Astrid, I can't tell you what a loser I felt like watching that poor kid walk down the jetway, the weight of the world on her thin little shoulders.

On the way home, I beat up my steering wheel, banging it with my hands, as I thought of all the ways I'd failed her. Why hadn't I let my wife drive her? Cassie had wanted to (and would have been much better with Caroline) but was scheduled to take the other girls out on the trail for the big "female fiesta" campout, and I told her we couldn't disappoint them. I should have realized that grief trumps disappointment. And then, why hadn't I been brave enough to talk, even after Caroline shushed me? I was the adult, I was in charge, yet I was kind of relieved when she spared me the burden of trying to find the right words to say. And finally, why did I force her to get on the plane? It might have messed things up a little, but couldn't I have gotten her on a later flight, when she was just a little more ready?

As I was talking to her on the telephone, I thought of good idea number three (all by myself!), which was inviting her to the ranch for Christmas. I thought it might be good for her—and good for me in that now, finally, I could be of some help.

She didn't say yes but she didn't say no.

Your friend,

Cyril

8:24 p.m.  December 15, 20—
To: dfarms@azlinx.com
From: isleast@nsd.com
Subject: Re: What do you think?


Dear Cyril,

I think asking Caroline to your ranch is a wonderful idea. It would do her a world of good and I hope she says yes.

I'm in a good mood today after having gotten a surprise Christmas present in the mail. I had complained to a company that manufactures some of my favorite cookies (I don't know if I've bragged to you about my baking skills, but they're prodigious; however, I think the Scots know a secret to shortbread that I'm not privy to) and hadn't gotten a reply. I assumed my complaints had fallen on deaf ears, as complaints do so often these days.

But my faithful postman, who's especially eager to make the trek out to the island during the holiday season (he never leaves without a coffee-and-cookie break), delivered me a package with a distinctive plaid logo on the return address label, and when I opened it up, there was a big tin of pistachio-coated chocolate-dipped shortbread cookies, all artfully arranged, with no cellophane. You see, my letter of complaint had to do with their overpackaging.

The enclosed letter thanked me for being a loyal customer and especially for giving suggestions as to how to improve their product. They decided to return to their old way of packaging—sans cellophane—and hoped that I enjoyed the cookies as well as the knowledge that my complaint had made a difference!

I suppose it's all about making things better . . . from the packaging of shortbread cookies to the repackaging of our Caroline.

Your friend,

Astrid

*2:18 p.m. December 15, 20—*
*To: isleast@nsd.com*
*From: caro@dix.org*
*Subject: An offer I can't refuse?*

*Hey Astrid,*

*Your lilting voice is still in my head and it still soothes me the way it always did. Maybe if all UN translators had Scandinavian accents it would help the peace process; I mean, how could country X's threats be taken seriously by country Y if they were given in an accent that sounds like a song? So whaddaya think—should I send my idea to the secretary of state?*

*But your voice isn't the only one I'm thinking about—Cyril called me up just a few hours ago! I imagined his voice had aged into one like an old movie cowboy's, raspy and full of yodels, but it was clear as I remember it, and in its monotone way (at least compared to yours) comforting. He asked me to come to the ranch, promising horseback rides, campfires, and, most of all, privacy. He says he can't promise me snow, but he wouldn't be surprised if there is some.*

*What do you think? I'm tempted but scared. Scared of what, I'm not exactly sure, only I find I'm scared when considering most everything. I don't know whether this is something new or if I've always been scared but covered it up with alcohol.*

*The trees across the street look as if they've been swiped with a lacquer of ice. The sky is gray and heavy, as if it's ready to drop a load of snow. I'd love to be out there, and so would the gang of picture takers who still wait for me.*

*Love,*

*Caroline*

*P.S. I leave this radio station on that plays Christmas carols and just heard "Silent Night." Remember?*

9:41 p.m. December 15, 20—
To: caro@dix.org
From: isleast@nsd.com
Subject: Re: An offer I can't refuse?

*Min kjaer* Caroline,

I have been sitting at my little desk, staring out at the sea, but seeing only the memory "Silent Night" brought back.

You and I were stuck in a spooky Bavarian castle watching a Tom Jones Christmas special while a blizzard rattled the windowpanes. It seems funny now, but I remember how abandoned both of us felt—you by your parents (who'd gone shopping in Munich that afternoon with our German hosts and were waiting for the weather to clear to come back) and me by my old life. I was just three weeks into the job and now I was supposed to entertain you on Christmas Eve?

I was telling you how in my family, Christmas Eve was the bigger celebration; we opened our presents on Christmas Eve.

"What about Santa Claus?" you asked, and I told you we'd been brought up not to believe in Santa Claus. Your response was, "Bummer."

That very word seemed to pour over us like a gray mist, and we sat on that opulent yet uncomfortable couch staring at the television, miserable.

Our hosts had given most of the servants the holiday off except for the butler, Johann, who was vaguely jaundiced. He scared us both, and we jumped when he came into the room, leaning on the tea cart as if it were his walker. I thought there was a baleful expression on his long yellow face, and as he poured our tea we both watched carefully, barely breathing, expecting him to do something sinister. There was a squeal of wind and then, in a very soft voice, Johann starting singing, in a thick German accent, along with Tom Jones.

We looked at each other first in astonishment and then in delight—in fact, that's when we coined our word *schnizzle-boggled,* right?—and Johann, offering us a sly little smile, set down the silver teapot and began to dance. He was tall and stooped, and did the twist as he sang "It's Not Unusual," and as we laughed and clapped, he extended his yellowed hands to us and we got off the couch and danced with him. When the song was over and another began, we danced to that one too, but while Johann might have had the soul of Mr. Jones, he didn't have the stamina, and we made him sit down. You ran and got another cup and saucer from the kitchen and you served the old butler tea and then peeled him an orange, and from the look on his face, one would have thought gold had been laid at his feet.

We ate orange sections and lebenkuchen and drank tea, and Tom Jones was replaced by a church service. When a soloist sang "Stille Nacht," Johann sang along in German, and you joined in in English and I in Norwegian.

Your parents got home the next morning, with presents galore, and at dinner that evening, when Johann served the roast duck and potatoes, you quietly hummed the first few bars of "It's Not Unusual." The dour expression on his long yellow face didn't change, but on the way back to the kitchen, he shook his hips, just enough for you and me to notice.

What schnizzlebogglement!

XXX

Astrid

*8:15 a.m. December 16, 20—*
*To: isleast@nsd.com*
*From: caro@dix.org*
*Subject: Re: Re: An offer I can't refuse?*

*Oh, Astrid—Johann! Do you suppose he's still living? I love when people do what you don't expect, especially when that thing is so fun, so* gracious.

*Thanks for taking me down memory lane to those times that are so nice to revisit. Do you remember our one New Year's Eve together? Dad and Mum were off ringing in the new year with heads of state or kings and queens or whomever they thought it beneficial to ring in the new year with, and you and I had returned from Germany to Portugal. A package had arrived addressed to me and was unopened under the tree. It was from an old business associate of Daddy's, and it was a bunch of coloring books and crayons and a couple of dolls. Obviously he had misjudged the age of the daughter of the man he wanted favors from.*

*While everyone was out at parties, we were sitting at the formal dining room table coloring away, listening to classical music. Sometimes we'd share a book as we colored, you on one page and me on the other. One was a Sleeping Beauty coloring book, remember? You laughed when I colored her hair gray, and I ex-*

plained it only made sense, because she'd been asleep for a long time. When the big clock donged midnight, we were surprised, and you apologized because we had planned to watch the countdown on TV, but I hadn't cared; coloring in *Sleeping Beauty* and *Hansel and Gretel* and *Barbie and Ken* coloring books and drinking hot chocolate and listening to the Berlin Orchestra on the radio was one of the nicest New Year's Eves I'd ever had.

More schnizzlebogglement!

Caro

8:51 p.m. December 16, 20—
To: revbill@reacres.com
From: dfarms@azlinx.com
Subject: A change of plans

Dear Bill,

Good hearing your voice this evening. I really appreciate you and Bev wanting to include me for Christmas
and I know I said yes, but . . . well, you more than
anyone else know how things change. So I guess I
won't be coming out to Arkansas after all.

Now, before you get all hot under the collar (now that
you're retired, are you still wearing that thing?), let
me tell you that I'm staying here not to keep away
from whatever pretty little widow you've also conve-
niently invited, but for the greater good. And that's
what you always preached, isn't it, Bill—acting for the
greater good?

Caroline Dixon just called to tell me she's taking me up
on my offer. I'll be picking her up in Flagstaff tomorrow.

I'm going to try to give that poor girl something she
hasn't had in a long time—a safe haven—so I've got

work to do. There's a stinky, arthritic dog to bathe, a guest bedroom to make up, and beans to soak for to-morrow's chili. You can't shortchange someone on her haven!

Cyril

*8:00 a.m. December 17, 20—*
*To: dfarms@azlinx.com*
*From: revbill@reacres.com*
*Subject: Re: A change of plans*

*Dear Cyril,*

*We didn't invite a pretty little widow—she's a cute divorcée.*

*I'll excuse you this time, but only because I'm a sucker for the greater good. I think it's wonderful that you're reaching out to Ms. Dixon. God knows (literally) she could use a helping hand.*

*As your church attendance has been lax of late (yes, Pastor Storby keeps me posted on your attendance), I'm pleased to see you've formed your own outreach committee. The funny thing is, reaching out always benefits the one who offers the hand as much as the one who takes it.*

*Give Paul and Theresa my love when you talk to them.*

*In peace,*

*Bill*

From the "Here's Buzz" column in *Star Gazer* magazine, December 18, 20—

Silver bells. . . that's what rock 'n' roller **Jersey Slade** bought for yoga workout czarina **Svetlana Roloff**, big silver bell earrings to wear when she gets tired of the gold ones!

"Christmas is the perfect time for me." said the diminutive drummer, " 'cause I love to buy her presents."

"Ho ho ho," responds his not-quite divorced wife, makeup artist **Annie Slade.** "After my attorney gets through with him, he won't have enough money to buy her a yoga mat."

Old and new Hollywood came out for the funeral of director **Mo Preski.** Mr. Preski is most famous for his violent 1970s psychothriller *Santa's Got a Gun,* which still attracts audiences at midnight screenings, but in fact Preski made several critically praised documentaries, even winning an Oscar for his biopic of female track stars, *Beware of Fast Women.* In a bizarre twist, he was killed while riding his bike along the Santa Monica Strand, from injuries sustained after a woman out for a run knocked him over.

Well, the holidays are in full swing and yours truly hopes you're swinging with them. And for those of you who find yourselves, for whatever reason, depressed at this time of year, remember: there's always eggnog.

While you're rushing home with your treasures, don't forget—you've only got one more week to cast your vote for America's Most Unadmired Man and Woman.

3:13 p.m.  December 18, 20—
To: thebuzz@sg.com
From: dfarms@azlinx.com
Subject: Small favors


Dear Mr. Buzz,

Well, to be fair, I guess I should write you when I'm *not* mad at you. Thanks for not ragging on Caroline Dixon in your latest column.

Merry Christmas.

Cyril Dale

4:32 p.m.  December 18, 20—
To: dfarms@azlinx.com
From: thebuzz@sg.com
Subject: Re: Small favors


Dear Mr. Dale,

You're welcome—but don't think I've had a conversion or anything. It was just a slow news week.

Thanks for the Christmas wishes, but like I said, I don't celebrate the holiday.

The Buzz

*11:48 a.m. December 20, 20—*
*To: isleast@nsd.com*
*From: caro@dix.org*
*Subject: Here I am!*

*Well, Astrid, as the subject line says, here I am! And where's that? Oh, on a wide-open porch, sitting on a rocking chair, looking out at an empty bunkhouse (the one I stayed in years ago), a ridge of mountains, and a corral in which two horses and Flipper—the cutest colt ever—are romping and stomping and snorting. Cyril is out in the barn, and Astrid, he's greezan well, for an old guy. He's hardly changed at all—still the tall and lanky cowboy, although his hair's silver now. And he has the kindest brown eyes.*

*Thanks to the concierge at the Pierre, who arranged a red-headed decoy (can you believe it?), I got out of there without much trouble. I hired a private jet and flew into Flagstaff, so at least for now (knock on wood) it really does seem like I'm living incognito. Yippee! Sitting out in all this quiet openness . . . I feel so free. Yippee again! (Hey—maybe that's the genesis of the word yippee—the verbalization of a cowboy's jubilance at being out on the range!)*

*Cyril met me at the airport with a poinsettia plant (!) and a big hug. I thought it was going to be a little awkward, and it was, es-*

*pecially as we were walking to the car, but when he put my bags in the trunk he said, "Caroline, whatever you want, whenever you want it, you just ask me. I'm here to help."*

*Of course I teared up, until he added, "Well, not whatever . . . and not whenever, but you get the picture."*

*We both laughed, and by the time we were on the road, it was easy to see that our friendship wasn't going to be confined to cyberspace. Friends! Isn't it funny how I could have a hundred people show up at one of my parties and if I trolled through the crowd, I couldn't find one real friend? I think of my years away at school after my dad died and how I fought friendships; how it just seemed easier to put up a shell. I was like a june bug, with a hard shell protecting those soft places where love can sneak in and ultimately sting. Later, when I became "known," everybody wanted to be my "friend," and I collected these friends the way I would accessories: who complements me? But as weird as this sounds, I don't think I have closer friends now than you and Cyril. And my sponsor, but in her friendship, I feel like I'm doing all the taking, whereas with you guys, it's a give-and-take. I hope you feel the same way, because it's so nice to be worried about someone else's feelings for a change!*

*Astrid, even though my sponsor hears the most about my darker feelings, I think I've expressed some of them to you . . . how edgy*

*I feel sometimes, so uncertain that I can be anything other than what I was. But right now, I FEEL GOOD!*

*I slept under a pieced quilt in a split-log-framed bed, and I can't tell you when I've had a better night's sleep. Now I'm on the porch, wearing a plaid wool jacket Cyril said was Cassie's, looking up from this to see the horses puff steam out their big velvet nostrils.*

*And Cyril says the clouds that are blowing in from the north could just as soon have snow in them as not. So I'll say it again, podner: yippee!*

*XXXOOO*

*Caroline!*

10:15 a.m. December 19, 20—
To: caro@dix.org
From: asmythe@WOC.org
Subject: Thank you


Dear Caroline:

On behalf of everyone here at World of Change,
I'd like to thank you for your very generous
year-end check. As you know, we're hoping step
by step, girl by girl, woman by woman, to change
this world of ours for the better.

A personal note, Caroline—we really were going
to change the focus of our advertising before
your "incident." I understand you've taken
steps to change your own world, and to that I
say bravo! And Merry Christmas!

Agatha Smythe

10:16 p.m. December 20, 20—
To: isleast@nsd.com
From: dfarms@azlinx.com
Subject: Why not?


Dear Astrid,

Both Caroline and I really enjoyed talking to you tonight. Your voice hasn't changed much in thirteen years—you still sound Swedish! When she was on the phone with you, Caroline's face shone with one thing: happiness. Boy, it did my heart good seeing that.

Earlier my son, Paul, had called from Africa, and I asked him to say hello to her too. I'm so proud of Paul, and I thought it would be nice for her to talk to a guy like him. Then I realized, with a little surprise, that I was proud of her and thought it would be nice for him to talk to a gal like her.

Astrid, like I said, you sound like Inger Stevens, but I also thought I heard a little loneliness in your voice, so I was thinking: why don't you come here for Christmas? I don't know if you've ever seen northern Arizona, but it is beautiful in ways you can't imagine. Now, I don't know much about your family in Norway, and maybe you've got a big to-do planned with them, but whatever your plans, I want you to seriously consider my invitation. I think it would be great for Caroline, and I'd sure like to meet my "partner in crime."

Think about it. We've only got store-bought Christmas cookies around here.

Cyril

*11:04 p.m. December 20, 20—*
*To: caro@dix.org*
*From: gillh@lonsw.com*
*Subject: Happy holidays*


*Dear Caroline,*

*It sounds as if you're making some real progress—your voice sounds so clear on the telephone! Mummy and I are so very happy for you.*

*Perhaps we'll find some time in the New Year to get together?*

*Fondly,*

*Gillian*

1:10 p.m.  December 20, 20—
To: caro@dix.org
From: bs@mgf.com
Subject: News


Caro—

I hear through the grapevine you've put the booze away.
Congratulations, although as the new VP of sales of Maestro
Liquor, I feel sorry for our lost income—ha ha!

You might have heard I'm engaged to Ellie Lange. Her father
was more than happy to welcome me aboard Maestro, and
I'm happy to be here. Maestro's got a lot of interests besides
liquor (what could be more interesting than that, you're
probably wondering? Ha ha), and I'm hoping to get into the
movie production end of things fairly soon.

Ellie and I just bought an apartment in Trump Tower and
things are looking great. I'd invite you to the wedding, but
Ellie doesn't want any brawling—ha ha!

Anyway, Merry Christmas.

Bradley Somerset

*8:13 a.m.  December 21, 20—*
*To: isleast@nsd.com*
*From: caro@dix.org*
*Subject: Reunion*

*Astrid—*

*I just got in from riding the horse I rode thirteen years ago! A big gentle chestnut mare named Sosie who made me feel I wasn't a complete city slicker. (I think I might be the only one on the "heiress circuit" who didn't start riding when she was two!) Then I played with the colt—I run outside the corral and he condescends to run alongside me for a little while before turning up the heat and leaving me in the dust.*

*Some "white precipitation" today (who'd have thought of snow in Arizona?), but nothing's stuck to the ground yet. Doesn't matter—it's really beginning to feel like CHRISTMAS. Oh, Astrid, Cyril told me of his invitation—PLEASE PLEASE PLEASE PLEASE PLEASE take him up on it—it would be so schnizzle-boggled!*

*So get on the Internet and order your plane ticket—now!*

*Love, love,*
*Caroline*

*P.S. You'd be proud of me—I heard from a former (thank God) boyfriend of mine who reminded me of how cloudy my judgment was when I drank. I was about to return his snotty e-mail with one of my own when I thought, nope, I'm past that. Well, at least right now—tomorrow I might fire off the meanest e-mail ever written.*

*P.P.S. Have you got that plane ticket yet?*

2:34 p.m.  December 21, 20—
To: mberg@cal.com
From: lw@wpalms.com
Subject: Who else?


Dear Mitch,

Here's the conversation that went on after your grand-
mother asked why we weren't going Christmas caroling.

"Because we're Jewish, Mama," said your mother.

"But I want to put on a hat and mittens and sing outside in
the snow!"

"Mama, we live in Florida."

"Don't be so negative, Rachel."

Thought you'd enjoy that.

Lorraine

5:50 p.m.  December 21, 20—
To: revbill@reacres.com
From: dfarms@azlinx.com
Subject: Boy oh boy


Dear Rev,

So, what's a Hot Springs Christmas look like? Bet it
can't top this one . . . although I'm sure the Lord's
done masterful work out there too. I just sort of look
at Arizona like the Mona Lisa in the Louvre—she's the
top draw for good reason, wouldn't you say?

Caroline and I dragged the tree out of storage and
put it up. She was surprised that we didn't go chop
down one, but I told her how Cassie was a reuser/
recycler from way back, liking the idea of our "real"
Christmas tree being out there somewhere in the for-
est, with a redbird or two perched on its branches,
singing.

I told her how Cass would always put bunches of sage
around the house so that instead of a traditional
evergreen smell, our Christmas smell was "desert traditional."

Bill, I don't know if you and Bev still put up a tree with all the ornaments you've saved from when your kids were young, but man, if that doesn't put a lump bigger than a golf ball in your throat! Caroline inspected each pipe cleaner candy cane and baked clay Santa the way a jeweler inspects a diamond—holding them this way and that, turning them slowly. I laughed and said a person would think she'd never seen a homemade ornament, and she said that she really hadn't. She said her family's Christmas ornaments were so delicate—and so expensive—that she wasn't even allowed to trim the tree! Man, what's the matter with those people?

I'm so glad she's here, Bill. We had a winter campfire last night, and the clouds had blown away (delivering maybe two flakes of snow), so the stars were out. She asked me all about Cassie and let me talk as long as I wanted (and it was a long time). It was funny, though—you know how stingy I've been with those stories, hoping to avoid that sharp pang in my heart, that sensation of having to turn around quick just in case she might be there and I could grab her. Well, there was none of that. Just kind of a warmth, like a pat on the back, only it was inside my chest. I kind of thought it was Cassie, telling me everything—everything!—was okay.

I'm still hoping Theresa and Rich are going to make it down from Alaska, but she hasn't said as much. Caroline and I thought it would be a great idea to ask Astrid, my co-conspirator in the Save Caroline campaign (not that it was us who saved her), to join us, and we called her again today but so far haven't gotten a yes. Still, like you advised, I'm reaching out, and who knows how far that reach might take me?

You can read into that whatever you want.

Cyril

P.S. Love to Bev and that cute divorcée.

6:30 p.m. December 21, 20—
To: caro@dix.org
From: gwms@holstu.com
Subject: Merry Christmas


Hi Caro—

Is it tacky to have Xmas cards with your name embossed on them? They said no at the printers, but I figure you know more about things like that than some printer. Anyways, I can't send you one since you won't tell me where you are, but I can at least send you a Merry Xmas by e-mail.

I'm doing a movie in Mexico City in January. I'm supposed to be this Mexican wallflower who blossoms into this world-renowed flamingo dancer, so I'm supposed to gain fifteen pounds (for when I'm a wallflower)! Eating a lot of tacos and stuff, trying to get myself in caracter!

Anyway, thanks for those cards and calls. Sorry it took me a while to answer them. But you know how it goes. Busy, busy, plus I was still sort of mad. But the new years coming and I always like to start fresh, so maybe we can get together before I go to Mexico! Beware, thou—my hair will be dyed black, and I'll be a little (a lot) fatter.

Anyway, have a merry Christmas and happy new year, and I'm happy for you!

Gina

10:04 p.m. December 21, 20—
To: isleast@nsd.com
From: mbc@ebpub.com
Subject: Give yourself one


Dear Astrid,

I know I told you all this on the phone, but I want you to see this message when you wake up and open your computer:

# For God's sake—go!

We have been friends for nearly twenty years and I know I've given you a lot of advice, but believe me, you've required a lot. Seriously, you have to have more friends than just me, Astrid. These people need you and you need them. Stop keeping secrets that shouldn't even be secrets! Stop being so scared to live a life you deserve! Give yourself a break!

I mean it,

Meg

6:06 a.m.  December 22, 20—
To: dfarms@azlinx.com
From: isleast@nsd.com
Subject: The reason for things

Dear Cyril,

It was good hearing from you and Caroline last night. I thank you so much for your invitation, but I never ever leave my island. I must do my shopping on the mainland and I will meet friends at the airport in Oslo, but these are the exceptions. Because you've become a trusted friend of mine, I will finally tell you why.

I don't know if Caroline's told you about my unlucky-in-love story. As unlucky-in-love stories go, it's not the most compelling one or the most original. However, it was mine, and the heartbreak I suffered was real, but that negative turned into a positive because it's the thing that led me to the Dixon household and Caroline. Cyril, I was devastated when they sent that poor girl away to school. I can't say that I felt I was her mother, but I certainly felt a great and loving bond, and that she wouldn't answer my letters or take my telephone calls cut a deep wound in me. But, when you're young, you're resilient, however heartbroken you may feel, and when Caroline's mother steered me toward another nanny position, I took it.

The Kvitruds were an American family. Mr. Kvitrud worked for a Dixon concern in London, but after I was hired the family moved back to their home in Minnesota. I began work when their little boy, Timothy, was two years old, and I spent two and a half happy years with him before Drew was born. The baby was just like his brother, sunny-natured and smiling, and I was in love with them both. The only shadow on my happiness was worrying about Caroline. Enquiries to her mother were met with a terse "She's fine," and I could only hope she was telling the truth.

The excitement I had with the Dixon family was lacking—there were no visits from world leaders, no sudden trips to Rome, Paris, or California, and most especially none of the drama a thirteen-year-old girl can't help creating—but my life with these small children was hectic, happy, and sweet.

Both boys were blond-haired and blue-eyed, and when I had them out people assumed I was their mother. I believe I was hired because of the family's Norwegian ancestry, and Mrs. Kvitrud requested that I speak to them in Norwegian. Timothy could already converse with me, and with a little Bergen accent to boot! He was very proud of his role as big brother and very gentle with the baby. He loved to sit on the rocker and hold him, all the while telling him about all the toys in the room and how they'd play soldiers and cowboys and astronauts when he got a little bigger. Drew would laugh and grab at his brother's ear or nose, and Timothy, laughing back, would assure him that yes, they'd play wrestlers too.

I had switched my day off when it happened. A writer whose first manuscript I'd done some work on in England was appearing at a bookstore in Minneapolis, and I was very interested in seeing him. Mrs. Kvitrud even loaned me her car. I remember backing out of the driveway, waving happily to Timothy, who stood in the backyard sandbox, dressed in the Batman costume I had sewn for him. I was so excited, fantasizing that maybe the writer would remember me and that we'd go out for a drink and, more important, a good literary talk afterward.

I had arrived early and had just seated myself in the front row and was reading the dust jacket of the author's latest book when a bookseller tapped me on the shoulder and asked if I was Astrid. When I said yes, she said I had a telephone call. (Cell phones weren't as ubiquitous as they are now.)

It was the family's housekeeper, telling me there'd been an accident and to what hospital I should go.

Cyril, it's been ten years, but I can still barely write these words, let alone say them. Timothy lay in a hospital bed, connected to as much machinery as there is in an ICU.

He'd jumped out of the sandbox, and with arms extended ran around the yard, pretending he could fly.

Suddenly, he said to his mother, *"Batman glemt kysse Astrid!"* and he raced around the side of the house to the front yard.

At just that moment, a young man in a nursery truck loaded with three young crabapple trees was driving down the street.

Mrs. Kvitrud, who'd been chasing after Timothy, heard the squeal of brakes and rounded the corner of the house at the same moment the truck hit her son.

Of course, there was great damage done to many: to the gardener, who cradled one of his trees that had fallen into the street, crying as the police interviewed him; to Timothy's parents; to the housekeeper, who had seen everything; and to me.

The Kvitruds let me keep vigil with them, and when the doctors said there was no hope for him, they let me kiss him one last time. That's all he had wanted, all Batman had wanted—to kiss Astrid! That was the reason for everything that happened.

The parents, in their own grief, still found the heart to not blame me and urged me to stay on, but I couldn't. As much as I felt the baby needed me, I was terrified I couldn't keep him safe, that I wouldn't notice a cough turning into pneumonia, wouldn't recognize that a colicky tummy was really a burst appendix. And so I retreated to the little island house that has been in my family since before Norway gained its independence, and for the first couple of years I would sit out on the rocks facing the sea, thinking it wouldn't be that hard to jump off them.

I had never planned to work with children, but I fell into my positions with the Dixons and with the Kvitruds, and loved each one of those children. Despite that love, I failed both Caroline and Timothy. I didn't want to tell this story to Caroline because I was so happy at getting a second chance to help her and didn't think her hearing my troubles would do that.

I know there's no thing as real safety in this world, but I have convinced myself that I am safe enough in my little house on my little island. At least safe from the world of love and all its complications and pain.

Astrid

*8:40 p.m. December 22, 20—*
*To: isleast@nsd.com*
*From: caro@dix.org*
*Subject: Fair is fair*

*Astrid,*

*Cyril let me read your e-mail and I don't even care if you're mad. I'm mad. It's not fair that I get to need you but you don't get to need me. It makes me feel like a child.*

*You need to be with us now. We need to be with you.*

*You are wrong about failing me. You never have. That's been my department. Please give me a second chance to help you.*

*Get on that plane.*

*Caroline*

11:42 a.m. December 22, 20—
To: dfarms@azlinx.com
From: thebuzz@sg.com
Subject: Taken aback


Dear Mr. Dale,

Whoa—I can't say much surprises me, but I will say your telephone message did. I've written down all of the information but I can't say one way or the other if I'll use it.

Nevertheless . . . I will certainly think about what you said.

Sincerely,

Mitch "The Buzz" Berg

1:01 p.m. December 22, 20—
To: revbill@reacres.com
From: dfarms@azlinx.com
Subject: Some thoughts


Hey Rev—

I know you and Bev are at choir practice. Remember
years back when Edith Czerbiak sang "O Holy Night"
and you had to press your lips together and play with
your sermon notes so you wouldn't break into the gig-
gles I had? How could a woman bellow in a bass voice
like that?

Theresa and Rich did get out of their commitments in
Anchorage and are here. Theresa and Caroline went
for a ride this morning and came back rosy-cheeked
and laughing. Now they're in the kitchen, banging pots
and cracking eggs and chattering, and I'm reminded
what a happy sound women in the kitchen make.
Man, I sound like an old coot sometimes, don't I?

So a lot of Christmas cheer around here, and it does
warm these cockles, but I'm worried about my friend
Astrid. I told you about the tragedy that did her in,

and have been thinking about why some people are done in by it and others aren't.

Now, don't get so excited that you get an infarction or something, but we're all going to Christmas Eve services. Caroline and I were riding Homer and Sosie and you know how easy conversation—or quiet—can be when you're riding with someone. Anyway, she'd been doing what you can't help but do in these parts—admiring the view—and she said, "It really does look like God took a paintbrush to those rocks," and I said in true cowboy fashion, "Yep." Then we got on the subject of religion, and Caroline said that in her family Sunday mornings were reserved for brunch and the reading of international papers. Sometimes she went with her mother to Anglican services at Christmas and Easter, but they never prayed at the dinner table, etc. She said she's always thought there's a "higher power" but finally she "feels" it, and it's like a force that's helping her make it, like someone holding her hand.

Whenever I heard the phrase "the faith of a child," I thought that's what I had—a faith I just accepted was there, true and sure as the morning sun. But that sun spent way too much time behind clouds after Cass died, and I was scared at times that it was gone for good.

You once preached that your faith was a ship that not only took you to God but protected you in turbulent waters. Cassie said her faith was like music and it was part of the way she looked at the world. Mine's been under cloud cover for a while, but I'm starting to feel that sun again.

We are strange and hopeful beings, aren't we?

Cyril

*7:04 p.m.  December 22, 20—*
*To: dfarms@azlinx.com*
*From: revbill@reacres.com*
*Subject: Re: Some thoughts*

*Dear Cyril,*

*It's never a good thing when a soloist singing a reverent song makes a preacher laugh. But you're right—with that voice, Edith could have guided ships into harbor.*

*I know Bev sent you our regulation Christmas card, Cyril, but I just wanted to add a few more thoughts, especially after your last e-mail.*

*As you can imagine, I've had many discussions about faith through the years. When I was in my first parish, a woman—a banker's wife, and probably the hoi-est of the hoi polloi in that small town—objected to our children's Christmas program when we called it "A Season of Faith."*

*"You spend too much time talking about faith," she complained.*

*"But faith gets you to God."*

"But God's there whether you believe in Him or not!"

"That statement," I said, "is a testament to your faith."

She left my office with a hrmmph, as if I had insulted her, and I remember their next pledge was significantly smaller than it had been the year before.

You reminded me of the banker's wife when I first came to All Glory—you knew exactly what you knew, and you were always heading up, with Richard Perkins, the faction of those who thought I was "too liberal." I enjoyed those arguments we had over the years, and apparently you did too—or at least you never decreased your pledge.

And then when you defended me against an angry letter Richard Perkins wrote in the monthly newsletter; well, I showed you how I'd framed your response, and in fact am looking at it on my desk now.

'I think the Reverend would just like us to think about some things in a way we might not have thought before. There's nobody saying you shouldn't go back to the way you were thinking—you don't give up your home when you take a trip, do you? You're just allowing yourself to take a different road, look at some different scenery.'

*We've been worried about you these last couple years, Cyril,*
*but in the past couple months I think you've gotten back in the*
*boat, heard the music, and felt the sun. I'm so glad.*

*Bill*

11:16 a.m.  December 23, 20—
To: caro@dix.org
From: katha@gpl.com
Subject: You really were the most fun


Dear Caroline,

Merry Christmas from Tahiti! Yes, I am sitting in my glass-bottomed hotel room, watching pink and yellow fish swim under me!

I don't know if you heard, but I'm Blake Brenner's personal assistant now. He's shooting a movie on Bora Bora, so here I am, usual perks of the trade.

He's not as bad as the press makes him out to be (who is?), but he's not the easiest guy to work with either. He's always stealing my hair products, and he has more spa treatments in a single week than I've had in the last five years!

I know I said not to contact me, but I appreciate that you did. You really were the most fun person I ever worked for, and the smartest. I hope things are getting better and better for you, and whenever you're back in L.A., please give me a call. We can go out for coffee.

I'm glad you're thinking of going back to school, and glad that you're writing. Even the things you wrote when you were drunk were more entertaining than what a lot of people write sober.

Well, I've gotta get to the beach—Blake's filming a scene, and I've got the *very* important job of holding the umbrella that protects his million-dollar face between takes.

Happy new year too. (And it sounds like it will be!)

Kathy

2:08 a.m. December 25, 20—
To: mbc@ebpub.com
From: isleast@nsd.com
Subject: Merry Christmas (!!?)


Hello Meg,

I imagine Gwenyth and Peter have torn through all their Christmas presents, leaving you and Alex submerged in gift wrap and helping yourselves to a second eggnog. Were that Christmas were so prosaic here!

It's still early—maybe Santa hasn't finished his delivery and he'll drop off something at this house that we all need. Some calm. Some understanding. Some common courtesy.

I'm just fuming, Meg, and since I can hardly sleep, I'm going to unburden myself to you . . . Merry Christmas!

Things had started off so well, even though 'anxious' can't begin to describe my feelings on the plane ride over. Cyril picked me up at the airport—oh, Meg, he really does look like a cowboy!—and we were a bit giddy on the ride to the ranch, both of us so excited to surprise Caroline. And was she surprised! Our hug lasted a long time, and Meg, I never felt so *at home*. We had a beautiful morning; she and Cyril showed me around the ranch and even got me up on a horse. I rode around the corral, giggling like mad. I know the words *canter* and *trot* and even *run,* but what my horse was doing was *ambling,* and that was fast enough for me!

Along with Cyril's daughter Theresa and her husband, Rich, we worked all afternoon on Christmas Eve dinner, the men handling the bird and stuffing and the women the other side dishes, including, at Caroline's request, my cinnamon cookies. Cyril said it had been a long time since his kitchen had smelled so good.

What a dinner we had! Roast goose and all the trimmings and stories and laughter, and afterward we all climbed into Cyril's old van and drove to church. Now, you know a church is not usually where I find comfort, let alone joy, but this small wooden church, with its swags of pine boughs and its enthusiastic organist, filled me with a real spirit of the season, a feeling of peace and contentment.

Oh, would that it had lasted. The last hymn was "Silent Night," and Caroline leaned in toward me and whispered, "Here's to Johann." I teared up then, either from memory or from the scent issuing from the woman in the pew ahead of me, whose perfume did battle with the odor of mothballs emanating from her mangy fur coat.

The drive home through the high desert—peace and contentment. The cocoa by the fire—peace and contentment. Then the doorbell rang, old Kirby thumped his tail, and the door opened to a dark-haired stranger. The introductions were made—goodbye to peace and contentment.

Our visitor is none other than Mitch Berg. No, the name meant nothing to me either, until Cyril explained who exactly Mitch Berg is. Mitch Berg, Meg, is the man behind "The Buzz," that vile column from that vile tabloid, and CYRIL INVITED HIM!

"I'm sorry," said Caroline after Cyril had made the introductions, "did you just say what I think you said?"

"Yes, I did," said Cyril, his voice rushed, "and I can understand the look on your face—on your face too," he said, glancing at me, "but I thought maybe if I invited Mitch here to meet you, Caroline, he could—"

Caroline was off the couch and out of the room in a flash, and I was right behind her.

We hunkered down in her room for a while, ignoring all the pleas on the other side of the door until they stopped.

Our refrain to each other was "I can't believe he'd do this!" Why would such a seemingly kind, level-headed person do such a thing?

I left Caroline's room about one in the morning and have been stewing in mine ever since. If you have any thoughts on all this, please relay them to me, and if I don't hear from you, I'll assume you're having the kind of Christmas one should have—happy, serene, and not checking e-mails.

Love,

Agitated Astrid

The wee hours of December 25

Shit. I can't say I've never felt bad on Christmas day—we lived on a block where ours was the only house *not* lit up like Vegas, and every year I could count on those damn Quinlan brothers across the street showing off the loot Santy had brought them (chemistry sets, ten-speeds, autographed base-balls)—but shit, even the way I felt the year they got surfboards *and* electric guitars is nothing like the way I feel now.

I've imagined myself in a lot of settings, but never one like the one I'm in now: inside a fucking bunkhouse with a little heater that spits occasional heat and a horseshoe nailed above the door! The night's black like it never gets in L.A., and if I tip my head I can see a big yellow moon floating in that blackness. Cyril brought out some brandy, and while it might have made me a little drunk, any mellowing effects have burned off and what I feel now is lousy.

When Cyril made me his offer—"come and meet Caroline and you'll see she's not the person you write about"—the first thing I thought was: *I've got the story of the year!* So how could I, diligent reporter that I am, *not* show up with a nice lit-tle taping device? Just for accuracy, your honor.

After a long hairy drive from the Flagstaff airport, during part of which I was stuck behind a lumber truck on a winding canyon road the width of a bowling lane, I was thrilled not only to have found the place but to have found the place *alive*. I knew my reception might be a little *strained,* but I couldn't imagine the look of sickened shock on Caroline Dixon's face and the way she raced out of the room followed by Astrid (turns out it's a friggin' correspondents reunion).

The weird thing was that before Astrid bolted, she said, "I wouldn't be surprised if he's wearing a secret camera or a tape recorder!"

Whoa. Busted. Of course I had to look all offended, and Cyril bought my look of offense and apologized, even though he added, "But you can probably understand why they think that way." I shook my head like, no, I couldn't understand it. The awkwardness was spreadable, and Cyril's daughter and son-in-law quickly said their goodnights.

Even though I knew I'd probably end up upside down in some fucking arroyo, I was going to get back in the rental and drive to Flagstaff, but Cyril insisted it was too late and I should stay in the bunkhouse.

"I've got a bed all made up for you," he said, then added, "But let's have a brandy first." He poured me one, then refilled his own glass and said, "To you, and the courage it took to come out here. Sorry you got such a bad reception."

Feeling like a total shit, my digital recorder silently recording away, I gulped down that brandy and had another.

And then, facing that mammoth fireplace, he told me the story of how he, Caroline, and Astrid got together, and I've got it all here in this little machine.

It was after two when he walked me to the bunkhouse, and I've been sitting here listening to what I recorded.

"I know you were just doing your job, but did you ever think maybe you were in the wrong line of work?"

"Hey," I said, "a public figure is a public figure."

"Why? Because you say they are? What has Caro done to be a public figure?"

This by the way, was said not in an accusatory tone but with genuine curiosity.

"Well, she's richer than most people. In fact, she's a fucking heiress!"

"Don't talk about her like that."

"Sorry."

He nodded, accepting my apology.

"But say she wasn't an heiress. Say she was an actress, someone who made her living by having an audience. Does that mean she has to have an audience even when she's not working—even when she's buying milk or tampons at the grocery store?"

I shrugged. "I just feed the world's curiosity."

Cyril laughed; I would have too, hearing someone say that.

"Do you feed it or demand that it's fed?"

"You're pretty philosophical for a cowboy."

"You're pretty inane for a writer."

"That's not a very nice thing to say." This I said cordially, feeling the brandy by then.

"That's exactly what I say to myself every time I read your column," said Cyril, equally cordial.

I could have stayed up a lot longer, but when Cyril called it a night and said he'd better show me to the bunkhouse, I couldn't argue.

So I've been sitting here with this horse blanket around my shoulders, listening to the spitting heater and our conversation, and if I've ever felt crappier, I can't remember when.

*7:47 a.m. December 25, 20—*
*To: katha@gpl.com*
*From: caro@dix.org*
*Subject: Re: You really were the most fun*

*Merry Christmas Kathy,*

*I picture you having a seaside breakfast, listening to Tahitian percussionists play their version of "Little Drummer Boy" as you admire the huge bonus check Blake Brenner has tucked under your mimosa glass. How do you picture me? Because let me tell you, Kathy, anything you could imagine could not come close to the real picture of my Christmas Day.*

*I just got in from riding—not the most unusual thing to do on Christmas, considering I'm on a horse ranch. But guess who I gave a riding lesson to? I'll give you a clue. he was a real greenhorn. He might have been on a horse many times before, but this was the first he'd been on that wasn't attached to a merry-go-round. Okay, second clue: out of all the people who've given me reason to dislike them, he has probably given me the most reasons. Have you guessed yet, or are those mimosas clouding your speculative abilities? Okay, if you've gotten out of your chaise longue, sit back on it: Mitch Berg, aka, "The Buzz." Yes, the guy whose credo is: when you don't have anything nice to say, say it about Caroline Dixon!*

*He came sauntering into the ranch house late last night, and Kathy, when I found out who he was, I felt worse than betrayed; I felt betrayed by a person I'd thought was truly, sincerely, and thoroughly on my side. Cyril is a real gentleman—sort of like the guy your boss played in* Orchid Summer, *only not so smarmy. As soon as I got to his ranch, I felt safe, so you can imagine how I felt when I learned he was the one who had invited Mitch.*

*Well, let me tell you, breakfast this morning was a pretty frosty affair. Both Astrid and I were making plans to leave the ranch when Cyril came in. We jumped on him—"How could you?" etc., etc.—but all he said, in his slow thoughtful way, was, "Everyone deserves a second chance—especially someone like Mitch."*

*"So why is it that you think the person he's been the cruelest to should be the one to give him that second chance?" said Astrid, so mad her lips were white.*

*After pouring himself a cup of coffee, Cyril pulled a chair up to the table and straddled it.*

*"I'm truly sorry," he said. "It was stupid of me not to warn you in advance—but I hadn't heard anything definite from Mitch, so I figured he wasn't coming. Still, I should have told you I'd invited him."*

Astrid folded her arms across her chest and glared at him.

"But why would you invite him here at Christmas?" she asked. "I thought this was going to be a holiday where we all got to know one another . . . and then you throw in this, this—"

"This enemy," I said, finishing her sentence. "Who else have you invited who hates me?"

Cyril's face sort of crumpled then, and a part of me felt bad for him, but a bigger part thought, "Good. Now you know what it feels like."

He rubbed his mouth with his thumb for a while before he spoke.

"For a long time," he said finally, "I considered myself a Christian. I went to church and read the Bible and prayed to God every night. But then Cassie died and . . . well, it was a lot harder to be what I thought was a Christian."

He took a sip of coffee, cradling the cup in his big hand.

"Which is to be kind to people, to give them the benefit of the doubt, to reach out to those in trouble."

"There are a lot of people in need," said Astrid, all huffy. "Why him?"

"I couldn't stand the guy," said Cyril softly. "It scared me how much I couldn't stand him, how mad I'd get at him." He shrugged. "Maybe I invited him so that he could see how wrong he was about Caroline, and I . . . I could see how wrong I was about him."

"And did you?" I asked.

Cyril stared into his cup for a moment. "We talked for a long time last night," he said, "and after a while it was easy to just see him as this guy Mitch and not 'The Buzz.'"

"But he is 'The Buzz,'" reminded Astrid. "I don't care what he's like as 'Mitch,'—as 'The Buzz' he did a lot of damage."

Speak of the devil—at this point, Kathy, the back door opened and in he walks.

"I, uh," he began, his eyes darting everywhere except in the vicinity of our own, "I'm going to be leaving now. . . . I just wanted to say I'm sorry if I . . . if I made any of you uncomfortable, and I'm, uh . . . sorry for intruding on your holidays."

There was a long, uncomfortable silence, and then—don't ask me why, Kathy—I asked him if he'd like to go for a horseback ride. He made a sound between a laugh and a cough and said he wasn't much of a cowboy, and I said, "That's all right, I'll give you a lesson," and then Astrid stared at me for a long while before saying how a person can't ride without eating a good breakfast, and so we invited Mitch Berg to sit down and Cyril got up and fried eggs and bacon and Astrid made more coffee. But even though we were acting so well-mannered, the weirdness of sitting across the table from 'The Buzz' got to be too much and I told him I'd get our horses ready and to meet me in the barn.

I saddled up Sosie for me and mild old Henry for Mitch.

Talk about awkwardness. Conversation between us was minimal, limited to sentences like "These are your reins" and "To stop, pull back," and before we even got out on the trail I'd wondered a hundred times why I'd asked him to ride with me. He was feeling as miserable as me, clearing his throat, beginning a sentence and then stopping, sighing

We rode for a good mile, s-l-o-w-l-y, until we got to a lookout point that gives you a wide view of red mesas and scrub pines and I heard Mitch say, "Wow."

I had to smile. "That's pretty much the general consensus."

"It's so red," he said, looking out at the mesas. "It's beautiful."

"Cyril says it's sacred ground."

Henry snorted and shook his head, and Mitch gripped the saddle horn.

"Don't worry, he's not going to throw you," I said. "He's just a little impatient—I think he wants to get back to the barn and his hay." I turned Sosie around. "Shall we?"

"Sure," he said, and even though he pulled the reins in the wrong direction, Henry knows the way back to the barn with his eyes closed and turned the right way.

We rode in silence for a while until Mitch said something.

"What'd you say?" I asked, not hearing him.

He cleared his throat. "I said I'm not really an asshole."

"You just write like one?"

"You're not going to cut me any slack, are you?"

"Did you cut me any? Or my dad—bringing up that old scandal stuff? He was proven innocent, you know."

He looked pained, and I was glad. I gave Sosie a little nudge with my heels then and told her, "Giddyup!"

Henry's a docile horse, but he does love a good race, and despite Mitch's pleas to slow down, he wasn't about to let Sosie beat him back to the barn. I laughed nearly all the way home.

*More later.*

*Caro*

December 26, 20—

Dear Dad,

It was great talking to all of you—certainly sounds like you guys were having quite a party there. Or I guess I should say *are*, since I only hung up the phone and it's still Christmas Day where you are. I'm feeling decidedly lonesome, but in a good way—I guess you wouldn't be lonesome if something wasn't worth missing, huh? The villagers have been very kind in helping me celebrate; yesterday I had a big Christmas dinner (I'm finally used to all these spices!). Still, I'm thinking of how Mom would wake Theresa and me up by playing her guitar and singing "Santa Claus Is Coming to Town" and how we'd make a mad dash to the tree and our presents; how the house always smelled of evergreen and sage; the peanut butter treats Kirby would always get in his stocking; and the horse rides we'd take after Christmas dinner.

Wish I could be there to play our Christmas game with everyone.

Merry Christmas, Dad.

Love,

Paul

P.S. How do you like the improvised stationery? It's a math worksheet—look on the back and see if you can figure out any of the problems!

December 25, 20—
From Mitch Berg's recording device

*Caroline:* Check, check, is this on?

*Mitch:* It's on.

*Caroline:* Well, if anyone should know, it's you.

(Laughter)

*Caroline:* Okay, to set the scene, we're all sitting here in Cyril's great room on Christmas Day. The fire's blazing, we're inhaling Astrid's fabulous cookies and chugging eggnog, and we just talked to Cyril's son on the phone and he gave us a good idea as to how to put this tape recorder thing to *good* use.

*Mitch:* Mea culpa.

*Cyril:* Hey, let's give credit where credit is due. Our friend Mitch might have recorded us in secret, but he 'fessed up to it and swears he erased everything.

*Astrid:* He better have.

*Mitch:* On my honor.

*Astrid:* How much is that worth, Caroline?

(Laughter)

*Caroline:* Well, it is Christmas. So I guess he gets the holiday benefit of the doubt.

*Cyril:* So, like Caroline said, my son Paul called and reminded Theresa and me of the game we always played Christmas Day. We're going to play that game now and tape it for Paul—hi, Paul! Merry Christmas!—and send it to him either by mail or on the computer. You know how to do that, right, Mitch?

*Mitch:* I think I can figure it out.

*Theresa:* So it'll be sort of like you're here, Paul, playing along! I've already got the names in the bowl.

*Cyril:* Now everyone, take a name, and if you draw your own, throw it back. (Pause) All right, everyone got one?

(Chorus of yeses)

*Cyril:* Okay. What we do next is think a little bit about the person whose name we've drawn and then we write a fortune for them; a fortune we hope will come true by next Christmas.

*Astrid:* A fortune?

*Theresa:* Sure, something you hope will happen—or think needs to happen—to the person whose name you draw. Once Paul wrote that I would no longer be a tattletale and Mom wrote a whole song about Paul finding the gift of spontaneity. (Pause) Anyone want more eggnog? Mitch, you've hardly touched yours.

*Mitch:* Uh . . .

*Rich:* (laughing) I'm with you all the way, Mitch. There's a reason they only serve this stuff once a year.

*Theresa:* I'll make some coffee.

*Astrid:* I'll help you.

*Rich:* In that case, I wouldn't mind a few more of those cookies.

*Mitch:* Me neither.

*Theresa:* Oh, really? Well, they're on the kitchen counter. And while you're at it, why don't *you* make the coffee?

*Rich:* Yes, boss. Mitch, wanna help me out?

*Mitch:* More than anything.

*Theresa:* I think we should turn off this thing for now.

(Sounds of recorder being turned off and then on)

*Theresa:* Okay, Paul, we've stuffed ourselves with Astrid's cinnamon cookies and some fudge one of Dad's admirers brought over and everyone's written their fortunes and given them to me. Now I'm about to pass them out and we'll read them aloud. Okay, everyone take the one that has your name on it.

(Pause, rustle of papers)

*Theresa:* So who wants to go first?

*Cyril:* Go ahead, Resa. Show 'em how it's done.

*Theresa:* Okay, here's my fortune: "You will become a mayor's wife and quite possibly, a mayor's *expectant* wife."

*Cyril:* Hey! Is there something I should know?

*Theresa:* Yeah, is there, Rich?

*Rich:* You've been so patient with me, Theresa, willing to postpone what *you've* wanted . . . and I . . . well, maybe this year we should get serious about our progeny.

*Cyril:* Progeny—I like the sound of that!

*Theresa:* Me too! Wow—did you hear that, Paul? You might be an uncle sooner than you thought! (beat) Part of the game is to guess who wrote your fortune, and I think it's pretty obvious that Rich wrote mine. (Kissing sound) So now it's Rich's turn.

*Rich:* Okay. (rustle of paper) "A mayorship will be yours, but plans will be laid to lead you to the presidency." (beat) Wow. That's a pretty lofty fortune.

*Astrid:* And why not? You could certainly do better than what I've seen lately!

*Rich:* (laughing) Okay, I guess Astrid. Astrid wrote my fortune!

*Astrid:* Oh, I probably just gave it away! Sorry. But you're right, Rich, I wrote that. And I mean it too. You strike me as someone capable of running Anchorage . . . or America.

*Rich:* *Thanks.*

*Astrid:* But then again, so do you, Theresa.

*Theresa:* *Thanks.* (beat) So now it's your turn, Astrid.

*Astrid:* Oh, my. I'm a little nervous. (rustle of paper) "You will trade in your clogs for cowboy boots and extend your visa."

*Caroline:* (laughing) Astrid, you're blushing!

*Astrid:* No, I'm not, I'm . . .

*Theresa:* She's fanning herself, Paul.

*Rich:* So who do you think wrote that fortune, Astrid?

*Astrid:* (softly) I think Cyril did.

*Cyril:* Well, you're right. I did.

*Caroline:* You're blushing too!

*Cyril:* No. I don't blush.

*Theresa:* Then you've gotten a sudden case of sunburn, Dad.

*Cyril:* (coughs) So, anyway, now it's my turn. (rustle of paper) "Your relationships will expand; including a friendship with a cynical asshole." Hmm, the only person I can think of who'd use the words "cynical asshole" in a Christmas fortune is— well, it's gotta be you, Mitch.

*Mitch:* Sorry . . . I just wanted you to know how much I appreciate the way you . . . uh, reached out to me.

*Theresa:* But what do you mean by other 'relationships'? Are you talking about Astrid?

*Astrid:* Uff-da!

*Theresa:* Paul, you should know that for a non-blusher, Dad's all red-faced again, and so is Astrid.

*Mitch:* Why don't I go ahead and read mine, then.

*Rich:* (laughing) That's right, take the heat off ol' Cyril.

*Mitch:* (rustle of paper) "Your writing and your life will improve as you see what's really important." (pause) As much as the author sounds like Buddha or "The Little Prince," I'm going to have to say Caroline wrote this.

*Caroline:* I stand accused.

*Mitch:* And I guess I do too.

*Caroline* So what's your plea?

(Pause)

**Mitch:** "Guilty" . . . of being a prick sometimes and "not guilty" of being a prick at others. I'm sorry for the times I went out of my way to humiliate you, Caroline, but I can't apologize for those times I was just reporting on what you did.

**Caroline:** Half apology half accepted, Mitch. My question once again is why was it so important to report on what I did?

**Theresa:** Oh boy, might I remind you two that it's Christmas and you should save the fight for later?

**Cyril:** They're not fighting, Theresa, they're just working things out.

**Mitch:** That's right; we're just working things out. I am really sorry, Caroline, for all the hurt I caused you.

**Caroline:** I accept *that* apology wholeheartedly. And now I'll read my fortune. (rustle of paper) "Not only will your year be sober, but filled with people who care about the *real* you and not the you they think they know from the papers. P.S. The *real* you is much more interesting anyway." (beat) Since everyone but Theresa has already claimed to write a fortune, I pick Theresa.

**Theresa:** Man, you're sharp.

**Caroline:** Thanks. May I keep this?

*Theresa:* Be my guest.

(Pause, muffled noises)

*Theresa:* In case you're wondering what's going on, Paul, we all just gave each other a Christmas hug—and Caroline even hugged Mitch!

*Mitch:* (in pained voice) I don't know if the intent was to crack a couple of my ribs, but I appreciate the gesture!

11:14 a.m.  December 27, 20—
To: caro@dix.org
From: katha@gpl.com
Subject: Wowser!


Dear Caro—

Well, knock me over with an empty champagne bottle (not that you'd have any around). Mitch Berg aka "The Buzz," live and in person at the dude ranch? Sounds like a movie, and definitely better than the one I'm working on. Blake got stung by a jellyfish, and you would have thought a shark took a chunk out of him. His big toe's a little swollen, but that stopped production for three days. I'm beginning to think this six-week shoot might turn into a six-month one. Still, Tahiti    I can't complain

And neither can you, from your e-mails. I am so happy for you, Caro. I hope I get the chance to meet Cyril and Astrid and, dare I say, even Mitch. And is there someone I'm missing? . . . Oh, yeah, that teacher guy in Africa. The one you sound—hmmm, what's the word? Oh yes—*smitten* with. Or maybe I'm just misinterpreting all those exclamation points.

Anyway, Caro, you know your old pal Kathy is happy for you. When both you and I land somewhere, let's get together—but not for old times' sake. For new times' sake.

Uh-oh, Blake's calling—seems he needs his pacifier and lullaby . . .

XX

Kath

7:20 p.m. December 28, 20—
To: mcb@ebpub.com
From: isleast@nsd.com
Subject:

Dearest Meg,

I just got off the phone with Jan Kvitrud—well, actually I finished talking to her an hour ago, but it's taken this long for me to collect myself. Oh, Meg, I am so glad that I finally made contact!

I heard a gasp after I introduced myself and then a woman's voice asking, "Astrid, Astrid is that really you?" I began to apologize for my failure to communicate with them, but Jan cut me off, saying, "I'm so glad you're calling now!"

I told her what I'd been doing and she brought me up-to-date on their family, the big news being they had two more children, two little sisters for Drew.

"In fact Steven's got them all down at the ice rink—Drew and Hanna like to play hockey, and Astrid's our little speed skater!"

That's right, Meg: *Astrid,* although I can't say they named her after me entirely. Jan explained they'd always liked the name but she did add that once they got to know me, they liked the name even better!

Then, Meg, we had a very emotional conversation about Timothy, laughing and crying as we reminisced. Jan reminded me of the little green elf suit I had made for him and how he had continued wearing it after Christmas and into the New Year! I told her how I remembered how Drew had burst into tears the first time he saw Timothy wearing it and how Timothy picked up his baby brother and whispered something in his ear. The baby promptly quieted and later on I asked Timothy what he had said.

"He was scared because he didn't 'reccanize' me so I told him that even though I was Santa's helper, I was still Timothy."

Jan and I agreed that Timothy *was* Santa's helper, always ready to give whatever needed to be given.

Meg, my heart is so full I can barely stand it. Reconnecting with the Kvitruds is one reason why and the other is . . . well, shucks ma'am, seems I've fallen in love with a cowboy.

I don't know if I've given you any hints in my recent e-mails; apparently everyone here picked up pretty quickly what I wasn't sure I was ready to admit: I really care for this man! And Meg, the lovely part is that my feelings are reciprocated.

Cyril and I have gone for lots of long walks through this pretty country, talking about everything. Just yesterday, he was telling me more stories about Cassie, his wife.

"She was the one for me," he said, "no doubt about it. But she's gone now"—here he took my hand, Meg—"and I think she'd be the first one to say, 'So maybe Astrid's the one for you now.' "

I got a Christmas fortune that said I'd be trading in my clogs for cowboy boots and extending my visa. Looks like it came true.

Love,

Astrid

3:21 p.m. December 30, 20—
To: revbill@reacres.com
From: dfarms@azlinx.com
Subject: Schnizzlebogglement


Dear Bill,

Well, it's much quieter here than it was. Mitch flew to Florida after Christmas, Theresa and Rich went home Thursday ("Gotta hit the ol' campaign trail"), and we just got back from taking Caroline to the airport. First stop: New York for a few celebratory days with her sponsor. Then on to London to visit her sister and "mummy." We told her we'll be here if she needs us. She said she knows.

Had a long talk with Paul last night—or should I say Caroline did? My son's managing to get to a telephone a lot more these past couple days than he has during his whole time in Ghana! And sometimes Caroline passes me the phone and actually lets me talk to him! Oh well, that's a bill I won't mind paying.

Astrid doesn't know when she'll go back, but when she does, I'm going with her. I've never seen Norway, especially with a woman who looks—let alone talks—like

Inger Stevens. I know Cassie would approve because—
as you've reminded me—she kept telling me before
she died, "Don't close up, Cyril." I guess you've been
saying the same thing with all your widows and divor-
cées. . . .

I hear a tinny little tune playing—I can't really place it,
but I think it's supposed to be Arizona's state song.
It's from a music box Caroline got at Ye Olde Trading
Post when she and Theresa went shopping in town.
She gave it to Astrid to replace one she'd broken
years ago.

You should have seen the look that passed between
those two, Bill. I wondered who was going to break
down first. Then Astrid said, "You went shopping at Ye
Olde Trading Post and all I got was this lousy music
box?"

She's pretty funny for a Norwegian, but maybe you
had to be there.

Cyril

P.S. Don't be surprised if Astrid and I make a little side
trip to Hot Springs to tell you what the subject word
means.

*8:32 p.m. December 31, 20—*
*To: pf@htw.org*
*From: caro@dix.org*
*Subject: Happy new year!*

*Hey Paul,*

*I got to New York safely and am writing as you asked—although I'd probably write even if you hadn't asked. The streets are crowded with people, and some of them were paparazzi, but now I'm snugly tucked in my hotel room for the night. I'm prepared for a big celebration; I've got my bubbly water, room service, HBO, and a couple of coloring books. (I'll explain those to you some other time.)*

*One thing I learned in treatment is to trust your best instincts. I guess that means I might take you up on your offer to visit. I really want to figure out what I want to do next, and seeing someone who's sure and certain of his purpose might help. I'll be speaking to Agatha Smythe at World of Change when I'm in London; I think her program might have ways to work with yours.*

*It's been a long time since I've been so excited, Paul—excited and not afraid of what comes next. It feels as if it will really be a new year, with all of the old garbage dead and buried (well, at least bagged and ready for pickup). And don't laugh, but for the first time, this rich girl feels really* rich!

*Again, happy new year!*

*Caro*

*P.S. What's the weather like in Ghana these days? I want to pack like a traveler, not an heiress!*

From the "Here's Buzz" column in *Star Gazer* magazine, December 31, 20—

. . . Well, gentle readers, the new year is just hours away, and Yours Truly finds himself about to ring it in on the opposite side of the country. Yes, I've left the sunny climes of L.A. for the sunny climes of Florida, to throw out the old and ring in the new at the bedside of my dear **Bubbie**.

"Wait a second," you might be asking yourself, "what is this crap? Am I reading *Star Gazer*? Where's the gossip?" In time, in time; for now I ask your indulgence.

My Bubbie is a tiny little thing who had to wear high heels to clear five feet and would tease her hair to give herself a couple more inches. Then she doused herself in Emeraude just to make sure you wouldn't miss her. But she didn't need heels or a ratted beehive or Emeraude to let anyone know that she was the boss. She was a sharp career woman, working side by side with my grandfather in the furniture business, a fun and loving mother (who let my own mother and aunts do their homework on the store's recliners, remarking to customers, "These chairs build brains!"), and to her grandchildren our incomparable Bubbie. After school my sister and I would stop in at the furniture store and, from our own favorite recliners, talk to her about our day. Sometimes I would read her an essay or a story I'd written. Sometimes she'd say, "There isn't a grade high enough for that piece of genius." Sometimes she'd call out to my grandfather, "Saul, how old do you have to be to win a Pulitzer?"

It was easy to think you were pretty hot stuff with Bubbie in your corner.

She's old now (she'd get after me if I told you *how* old) and her mind takes a vacation as much as it stays put. Her glorious black beehive has long since whitened and deflated. She shouts out my name when I walk into her room, and two minutes later she asks me when the movie's going to start. Or if I'm home on leave. Or if I was interested in the dinette set with the oak or maple veneer.

But she was always, *always* in my corner. And over the holidays I was able to meet some people who, much to my surprise, seem to be in that corner as well.

So where am I going with this? When am I going to say the snide things about the depressive **Sharla Lincoln,** winner of *America's Best Vocalist,* who sings with so much angst that even her rendition of "Mary Had a Little Lamb" would cause us to wring our own necks? Or when am I going to mock the **Rev. Hap Humphries** for his plans to break ground for the Rapture Resort—"a vacation spot that'll give you a taste of what's in store"? And how about talk radio king **Speedy Cheddan**? When am I going to make jokes about his claim that he was taking cocaine as a scientist would, to study "that segment of society from an insider's point of view"? And how can I resist ridiculing **Blake Brenner,** who recently got hair extensions . . . on his chest?

I can't resist, and I'll do it all; I'll be as snide and mocking as need be (at least until my contract runs out). In this upcoming year, I resolve to keep writing and keep entertaining, because it's what I do best. I have lost my will to bully but not to opine; I will gladly, happily, and salaciously cover those who by their own efforts never cease to make a mockery of themselves. I will not, however, report on celebrities whom the media created only to knock them down. I might be a little kinder to people who might not have had a Bubbie in their corner. My grandmother would like that. She likes to laugh, but she likes to play fair.

And as for the winner of the Most Unadmired Man and Woman in America contest? Thousands of you voted, and some of those mentioned above received your votes. But it was a contest that ultimately had no winners, and to announce one would hinder that which the Buzz has resolved to be: better.

If you're disappointed, well, sorry . . . but not really. Maybe the next poll I'll hold is one that asks you to pick the Most Admired Man and Woman in America. Who knows—maybe the resolutions you make today will make you a worthy candidate. Good luck—I have faith in you. Hell, it seems I've got faith in all of us. After all, 'tis the season.

## Acknowledgments

To lovely Miss Carlson, my first-grade teacher who gave me the gift of reading ("See Puff jump!") and to the memory of Mr. Joseph Spaeth, who made me believe I could be a writer—I give you my deep thanks and hopes for huge salary increases for good teachers everywhere. To friends who've given me particularly good laughs this year, especially Kimberly (you're really something, girl!) and Kilian Hoffer, Wendy Smith, Dave Drentlaw, Judy Heneghan, Pete Staloch, Doug Anderson, Drew Jansen, Jimmy Martin, Renee Albert, Mike Sobota, and Lori Naslund, I give you the knowledge that fairy tales *do* come true for the young at heart. For excellence in publishing and representation, I give branch offices in Tahiti (mai tai lunches mandatory) to my editor, Linda Marrow; my agent, Suzanne Gluck; and their entire hard-working, creative, and good-looking teams. To the fantastic WWW, I give us fifty more years to solve the world's problems as we wine and dine together. To my book club, I give just as many years to talk about books and eat Doug Grina's superb food. To Wendy Haluptzok, a golden paintbrush for your artistry and enthusiasm. To Sissel Ilstad, free flights back and forth to Norway for arranging our own wonderful trip to the Homeland. Lots of chocolate to Lynn Ketelsen for the connections. Two baguettes and a case of Bordeaux to Jennifer Lund and Anne Gandrud, *mes amies qui parlent francais avec moi.* To Brenda Young and Terri Mickelson, for all the politically astute and entertaining e-mails; to Kirsten Ryden, Miriam Ramses, and Vellie Larson for the Norway help and to Laurie Kleven for the Greek lunches—a pound of lefse for being my cousins and aunt. For the Landviks: Wendell and Cindy, Lanny, Nichol, Adam and Amy, and Daisy, thanks for keeping our holiday traditions going—you have my permission to go ahead and splurge on my gifts. I give a daughter's love and gratitude to the memory of my dear dad, Glen, who laughed when he caught me sneaking peeks at the Christmas presents hidden in the closet, and to my dear mom, Ollie, whose exquisite sugar cookies and paper-thin krumkakka will never be matched. What I'd do for another chance to sit next to her at the piano and harmonize to "We Three Kings" or "Santa Claus Is Coming to Town."

## About the Author

LORNA LANDVIK is the bestselling author of *Patty Jane's House of Curl, Your Oasis on Flame Lake, The Tall Pine Polka, Welcome to the Great Mysterious, Angry Housewives Eating Bon Bons, Oh My Stars,* and *The View from Mount Joy.* She wishes everyone the best of the season—lots of comfort and joy and plenty of peace and love while we're at it.